22 DEAD
LITTLE
BODIES

By Stuart MacBride

The Logan McRae Novels
Cold Granite
Dying Light
Broken Skin
Flesh House
Blind Eye
Dark Blood
Shatter the Bones
Close to the Bone
22 Dead Little Bodies
The Missing and the Dead

The Ash Henderson Novels
Birthdays for the Dead
A Song for the Dying

Other Works
Sawbones (a novella)
12 Days of Winter (short stories)
Partners in Crime (Two Logan and Steel short stories)
The 45% Hangover (a Logan and Steel novella)
*The Completely Wholesome Adventures of Skeleton Bob
(a picture book)*

Writing as Stuart B. MacBride
Halfhead

Stuart MacBride

22 DEAD LITTLE BODIES

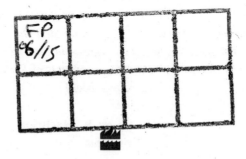

HarperCollins*Publishers*

HarperCollins*Publishers*
1 London Bridge Street
London SE1 9GF

www.harpercollins.co.uk

Published by HarperCollins*Publishers* 2015
3

A catalogue record for this book
is available from the British Library

ISBN: 978-0-00-812401-4

Typeset in Meridien by Palimpsest Book Production Ltd, Falkirk, Stirlingshire

Printed and bound in Great Britain by
Clays Ltd, St Ives plc

MIX
Paper from
responsible sources
FSC **FSC® C007454**
www.fsc.org

For Brucie

Without Whom

As always I relied on a lot of clever people while I was writing this book, so I'd like to take this opportunity to thank: Sergeant Bruce Crawford and everyone in B Division; Sarah, Jane, Julia, Louise, Oli, Laura, Roger, Kate (E), Oliver, Lucy, Damon, Charlie, Tom, Kate (S), Eleanor, Dom, Marie, the DC Bishopbriggs Pure-Dead-Brilliant Brigade, and everyone at HarperCollins, for doing such a great job; Lee, Graham, Angie, Pete, Lizzy, Chuck, Toby, Wayne, Liza, Kevin, Lorraine, Sarah, Charlie, Joe, Steph, David, Ann, Ross, James, Maggie, Susan, Chris, Joe and all the excellent booksellers and librarians out there – every one of you, most certainly, rock; Phil Patterson and the team at Marjacq Scripts, for keeping my cat in shoes all these years.

More thanks go to Allan, Lola, and Rudi for the feedback and input; Twinkle, Jean, Brenda, and Dolly Bellfield for the eggs; and Gherkin for the mice.

And saving the best for last – as always – Fiona and Grendel.

— one small step (one giant leap) —

1

Oh dear *God* ... it was a long way down.

Logan shuffled along the damp concrete ledge.

His left shoe skidded on something, wheeching out over the gaping drop. 'Aaagh...'

He grabbed at the handrail, heart thumping as the carrier bag from Markies spiralled away, down ... down ... down ... fluttering like a green plastic bat on a suicide run.

All the saliva disappeared from his mouth, leaving the taste of old batteries behind.

Thump.

The bag battered into the cobbled street: prawn-and-mayonnaise sandwich exploding, the bottle of Coke spraying foam out at the circle of onlookers. The ones nearest danced back a couple of paces, out of reach of the sticky brown foam. Then stared up at him again: a circle of pale faces and open mouths. Waiting.

One or two of them had their mobile phones out, filming. Probably hoping for something horrible to happen so they could post it on YouTube.

Had to be at *least* sixty feet down.

Why couldn't jumpers leap off bungalows? Why did the

selfish sods always threaten to throw themselves off bloody huge buildings?

Logan inched closer to the man standing at the far edge of the roof. 'You...' He cleared his throat, but it didn't shift the taste. 'You don't have to do this.'

The man didn't look around. One hand gripped the railing beside him, the skin stained dark red. Blood. It spread up his sleeve – turning the grey suit jacket almost black.

His other hand was just as bad. The sticky scarlet fingers were curled around a carving knife, the blade glinting against the pale grey sky. Black handle, eight-inch blade, the metal streaked with more red.

Great.

Because what was the point of slitting your wrists in the privacy of your own home when you could do it on top of a dirty big building in the east end of Aberdeen instead? With a nice big audience to watch you jump.

And it was a *long* way down.

Logan dragged his eyes away from the slick cobblestones. 'It isn't worth it.'

Another shrug. Mr Suicide's voice trembled, not much more than a broken whisper. 'How could she *do* that?'

'Why don't you put down the knife and come back inside?'

The distant wail of a siren cut through the drab afternoon.

'Knife...?' He turned his head and frowned. Little pointy nose, receding hairline, thin face, watery eyes lurking above bruise-coloured bags. A streak of dried blood across his forehead. The front of his shirt was soaked through with it, sticking to his pigeon chest. The sour stink of hot copper and rotting onions radiated out of him like tendrils.

Logan inched closer. 'Put it down, and we can go inside and talk about it, OK?'

He looked down at the carving knife in his hand, eyes

4

narrowing, forehead creasing. As if he'd never seen it before. 'Oh...'

'What's your name?'

'John.'

'OK, John: I'm Logan, and I'm going to— Bollocks.' His phone rang deep in his pocket, blaring out the Imperial March from *Star Wars*. He fumbled it out with one hand, the other still wrapped tightly around the railing. 'What?'

A smoky, gravelly voice burst from the earpiece. *'Where the hell are you?'* Detective Chief Inspector Steel. She sniffed. *'Supposed to be—'*

'I'm kinda busy right now...'

'I don't care if you're having a foursome with Doris Day, Natalie Portman, and a jar of Nutella – I'm hungry. Where's my sodding lunch?'

'I'm *busy*.' He held the phone against his chest. 'What's your last name, John?'

'What does it matter?' John went back to staring at the ground, blood dripping from his fingertips. 'Skinner. John Skinner.'

'Right.' Back to the phone, keeping his voice down. 'Run a PNC check on a John Skinner, IC-one male, mid-thirties. I need—'

'Do I look like your mum? Lunch, lunch, lunch, lunch—'

For God's sake.

'Just for *once*, can you think about someone other than your sodding self?' Logan pulled on a smile for the blood-soaked man teetering on the edge of the roof. 'Sorry, my boss is a bit...' He curled his lip. 'Well, you know.'

'And another thing – how come you've no' filled out the overtime returns yet? You got any idea—'

'I'm *busy*.' He thumbed the off button and stuck the phone back in his pocket. 'Come on, John, put the knife down. It'll be OK.'

'No.' John shook his head, wiped a hand across his glistening eyes, leaving a thick streak of scarlet behind, like warpaint. 'No it won't.' He held the knife out and dropped it.

The blade tumbled through the air then clattered against the cobbled street below.

A uniformed PC turned up, pushing the crowd back, widening the semicircle, looking up over her shoulder and talking into her airwave handset. With any luck there'd be a trained suicide negotiator on scene in a couple of minutes. And maybe the fire brigade with one of those big inflatable mattress things in case the negotiator didn't work. And this would all be someone else's problem.

'It'll never be OK again.' John let go of the railing. 'How could it?'

'Don't do anything you'll—'

'I'm sorry.' He crouched, leaned backwards ... then jumped, springing out from the roof. Eyes closed.

'NO!' Logan lunged, hand grasping the air where John Skinner wasn't any more.

Someone down there screamed.

John Skinner's suit jacket snapped and fluttered in the wind, arms windmilling, legs thrashing all the way down. Getting smaller, and smaller, and smaller, and *THUMP*.

A wet crunch. A spray of blood.

Body all twisted and broken, bright red seeping out onto the dark grey cobblestones. More screaming.

Logan crumpled back against the railing, holding on tight, and peered over the edge.

The ring of bystanders had flinched away as John Skinner hit, but now they were creeping closer again, phones held high to get a decent view over the heads of their fellow ghouls.

The wailing siren got closer, then a patrol car skidded to

a halt and four officers clambered out. Pushed their way through the amateur film crew. Then stood there staring at what was left of John Skinner.

Logan's mobile burst into the Imperial March again. Steel calling with the PNC check on their victim. He pulled the phone out. Pressed the button. 'You're too late.'

'Aye, see when I said, "Get your bumhole back here", I meant now. No' tomorrow, no' in a fortnight: now. *Sodding starving here.'*

2

'Where the hell have you been?' DCI Steel had commandeered his seat, slouching there with both feet up on his desk. A wrinkled wreck in a wrinkled suit, with a napkin tucked into the collar of her blue silk shirt. Tomato sauce smeared on either side of her mouth; the smoky scent of bacon thick in the air. She took another bite of the buttie in her hand, talking and chewing at the same time. 'Could've starved to death waiting for you.'

She'd made some sort of effort with her hair today – possibly with a garden strimmer. It stuck out at random angles, grey showing through in a thick line at the roots.

Logan dumped his coat on the hook beside the door. 'Feel free to sod off soon as you like.'

She swallowed. Pointed. 'You owe me a smoked-ham-and-mustard sandwich and a bottle of Coke. And change from a fiver.'

'They didn't have ham, so I got you prawn instead.' He scrubbed a hand over his face, then dug in his pockets. Dumped a couple of pound coins on the desk. 'Don't suppose there's any point asking you to get out of my seat?'

'Nope. Come on: make with the lunch.'

He settled into the visitor's chair, and slumped back, arms dangling loose at his sides. Frowning up at the ceiling. 'He's dead, by the way. In case you cared.'

'I'm still no' seeing any sandwiches here, Laz.'

'Ambulance crew say it'd be pretty much instantaneous. Flattened his skull like stamping on a cardboard box.'

'What about crisps?'

'Got you salt-and-vinegar. I slipped on the rooftop, almost went over myself. Lunch hit the deck instead of me. You can fight the seagulls for it.' He closed his eyes. 'They're probably busy eating leftover bits of John Skinner anyway.'

She sighed. 'See when they call it "talking a jumper down", they mean by the stairs, no' the quick way.'

'Funny.' He put both hands over his face. 'That's really, really funny.'

'Laz, you know I love you like a retarded wee brother, but it's time to pull up your frilly man-panties and get over it.' Steel's voice softened. 'People jump off things. They go splat. It happens. Nothing personal. Wasn't your fault.'

Raised voices thundered past in the corridor outside, something about football and beer.

'So…' A click, then a sooking noise. 'You got anything exciting on?'

He let his hands fall away. 'It's CID. There's *never* anything exciting on.'

Steel made a figure of eight with the e-cigarette in her hand. 'What did Aunty Roberta tell you?'

'Don't, OK? I'm not—'

'"Come join the MIT," I said. "These new specialist teams will hoover up all the interesting cases," I said. "All you'll be left with is the GED crap no one else wants to do," I said. "It won't be like it was when we were Grampian Police," I said. But would you listen?'

A rap on the door, then Constable Guthrie stuck his head

9

in. With his pale eyebrows, blond hair, and pink eyes he looked like a slightly startled rabbit. 'Sorry, Guv, but I need a word. Inspector?'

Steel popped the fake cigarette between her teeth. 'What?'

'Er, not you, Guv – DI McRae.'

She sniffed. 'No' good enough for you, am I?'

'It … I…' He pulled his mouth into a dead-fish pout. Then held out a sheet of A4 towards Logan. 'Did that PNC check you wanted: John Skinner, fourteen Buchanan Street, Kincorth. Married, two kids. Conviction for speeding eighteen months ago. Drives a dark blue BMW M5, registration number X—'

'Who cares what he drives?' Logan slumped further in his seat. 'We're not setting up a lookout request, Constable. We know fine well where he is.'

Pink bloomed on Guthrie's cheeks. 'Sorry, Guv.' He shuffled his feet a bit. 'Anyway, couple of people at the scene got the whole thing on their phones, you want to see the footage?'

'I caught the live show, I *really* don't need to see the action replay.'

'Oh…'

Steel polished off the last of her buttie, then sooked the sauce and flour off her fingers. 'Well, if you minions of CID will forgive me, I've got to go do some proper grown-up police work. Got a serial rapist on the books.' She stood and stretched, arms up, exposing a semicircle of pale stomach. Then slumped a bit. Had a scratch at one boob. 'Still hungry though.'

Guthrie pointed at his own cheek. 'You've got tomato sauce, right here.'

'Thanks.' She wiped it off with a thumb. 'And as a reward, you can get your pasty backside over to Buchanan Street, let the Merry Widow know her bloke's died of cobblestone poisoning. Offer her a shoulder to cry on – perchance a quickie, or kneetrembler up against the tumble drier – then wheech her down the mortuary to ID the body.'

Logan gritted his teeth. 'Do you have to be so bloody—'

'Oh come off it, Laz – the boy Skinner topped *himself*, no one made him do it. He jumped, leaving a wife and two wee kiddies to cope with the sticky aftermath. What kind of selfish scumbag does that?' Steel hoiked up her trousers. 'It's always some poor cow that's left picking up the pieces.'

And that's exactly what the Scenes Examination Branch had to do. Pick up the pieces before the seagulls got their beaks into what was left spread across the cobbles of Exchequer Row.

'… so I wondered if there was any news.' Logan paused in the middle of the corridor, one hand on the door through to the main CID office.

A sigh came from the mobile's earpiece. *'I'm sorry, Mr McRae, but Mr and Mrs Moore feel it's not really big enough for them.'*

'Oh.' His shoulders dipped an inch. He cleared his throat. 'Any other viewings coming up?'

'Sorry. Mrs Denis called to cancel Wednesday. They've bought a new-build out by Inverurie instead. The market isn't all that buoyant for one-bedroom flats right now.'

Great. Just – sodding – great.

'Yeah, thanks anyway.' The line went dead and he slipped the phone back in his pocket.

Eighteen months, and they'd achieved exactly bugger all.

He deflated a little further, then thunked his forehead off the CID door three times.

No reply. So Logan let himself in.

The main CID office wasn't anywhere near as big as the one they'd shared before the change to Police Scotland: no

11

big fancy flatscreen TV for briefings; no sink for making tea and coffee; no vending machine full of crisps, chocolate, and energy drinks. Instead, it was barely large enough to squeeze in four desks – one on each wall – and a pair of whiteboards covered in low-level crimes and lower-level criminals. A motley patchwork of manky carpet tiles clung to the concrete floor. Ceiling tiles stained like a toddler's nappy. Ancient computers with flickering screens.

Even the filing cabinets looked depressed.

Logan wandered over to one of them and checked the kettle perched on top: half empty. He stuck it on to boil. 'Where's everyone?'

DS Baird looked up from her screen. Pulled the earbuds out. 'Sorry, Guv?' Her short blonde hair formed random spikes on top of a rectangular face with heavy eyebrows. A pair of thick-framed glasses in black magnified her eyes to twice the size they should have been. Her smile was like a wee shiny gift. 'Coffee with two, if you're making.'

He pulled two mugs out of the top drawer. 'Where's Stoney and Wheezy Doug?'

She pointed at one of the empty desks. 'DC "couldn't find his own backside with both hands" Stone's off trying to find who's been vandalizing cars in Mannofield, and DC "just as useless" Andrews is off taking witness statements for that fire-raising at the Garthdee Asda.'

'You going to forgive them any time soon?'

'No. You need something?'

'Just interested.' The kettle rumbled to a boil.

'Hear you caught a jumper this afternoon.' Creases appeared between those thick black eyebrows. 'Well, not "caught" caught, but you know what I mean.'

'Guthrie's delivering the death message.'

A nod. 'I hate doing suicides. Don't mind telling someone their loved one's died in a car crash, or an accident, or they've been stabbed, but suicides…' Baird shuddered. 'It's the look of betrayal, you know?'

Logan dug a spoon into the coffee, breaking the kitty-litter clumps back into their individual grains. 'How many times do I have to tell people *not* to put damp spoons in the jar?'

'Like you're making it up to spite them.' A sigh. 'Can't really blame the family, though, can you?'

The office phone rang, and she picked it up. 'CID: DS Baird.' Then her expression curdled. 'Not *again* … Really? … Uh-huh…'

Two sugars in one mug, milk in the other.

'No. I can't … He's not here.'

Logan put the black coffee on her desk. She looked up and gave him a grimace in return. Put the phone against her chest, smothering the mouthpiece. 'Sorry, Guv, but Mrs Black's downstairs again.'

He took a sip of his own coffee. 'Which brave soul doth possess the Nutter Spoon of Doom upon this dark day?'

Baird scooted her chair over to DC Andrews's desk and pulled a wooden spoon from the top drawer. It had a photo of a woman's face stuck to the bowl end: grey hair, squinty eyes, long nose, mouth stretched out and down, as if she'd taken a bite out of something foul.

'Ooh…' Logan sooked a breath in through his teeth. 'Looks like it's not your lucky day, Denise, for whomever wields the Nutter Spoon of Doom must—'

'I'm on the no-go list. Apparently I'm in collusion with McLennan Homes and the Planning Department to launder drug money for the Taliban.' She held out the spoon with its glowering stuck-on face. 'Sorry, Guv.'

Logan backed away from it. 'Maybe someone in uniform could—'

'They're all banned from talking to her. She's got complaints in against everyone else.'

'Everyone?'

'Yes, but…' Baird waggled the spoon at him. 'Maybe she'll like you?'

Logan took the Nutter Spoon of Doom. It was only a little bit of wood with a photo Sellotaped to the end, but it felt as if it was carved from lead.

Oh joy.

3

Logan stopped outside the visiting-room door. Took a deep breath. Didn't open it.

The reception area was quiet. A bored PC slumped behind the bulletproof glass that topped the curved desk, poking away at a smartphone. Posters clarted the walls, warning against drug farms in cul-de-sacs and walking home alone at night. An information point cycled through views of Aberdeen. And a strange smell of mouldy cheese permeated the room.

No point putting it off any longer.

He shifted his grip on the thick manila folder tucked under his arm, opened the door, and stepped inside. It wasn't much bigger than a cupboard, with a couple of filing cabinets on one wall and a small opaque window that didn't really overlook the rear-podium car park.

Mrs Black was sitting on the other side of the small table that took up most of the available space. She narrowed her eyes, tugged at the hem of her skirt, and sniffed – turning that long nose up towards the ceiling. Her short grey hair shimmered as if it had been conditioned within an inch of its existence. Then the glasses came out of the bag clutched to her chest. Slipped on with all the pomp and circumstance of a royal wedding. Voice clipped and dark. 'I have been waiting here for nearly an *hour*.'

Logan suppressed a sigh. Did his best to keep his voice polite and neutral. 'Mrs Black.' Stepped inside and closed the visiting-room door. 'I'm sorry if my trying to catch criminals and keep the streets safe has inconvenienced you in any way.'

Her lips pursed. Pause. Two. Three. Four. 'He's doing it again.'

Of course he is.

Logan thumped the manila folder down on the little table. It was about as thick as a house brick, bulging with paper-work; a red elastic band wrapped around it to keep everything in. Then he settled into the room's remaining seat and took out his notebook. 'Right, we'd better take it from the beginning. You said, "He's doing it again." Who is?'

Mrs Black folded her arms across her chest and scowled. 'You know very well, "*Who*".' A small shudder. 'Justin Robson.' The name came out as if it tasted of sick. 'He's ... He's covering my cherry tree with ... *dog mess*.'

'Dog mess.'

'That's right: dog mess. I want him arrested.'

Logan tapped his pen against the folder. 'And you've seen him doing it?'

'Of course not. He's too careful for that. Does it in the middle of the night when Mr Black and I are sleeping.' Another shudder. 'Up till all hours listening to that horrible rap music of his, with all the swearing and violence. I've complained to the council, but do they do anything? Of course they don't.'

'You do know that we can't arrest someone without proof, don't you?'

Both hands slapped down on the desk. '*You* know he did it. *I* know he did it. Ever since I did my *public duty* and reported him he's been *completely* intolerable.'

'Ah yes.' Logan removed the elastic band and opened the folder. Took out the top chunk of paperwork. 'Here we are.

16

On the thirteenth of April, two years ago, you claimed to have seen Mr Robson smoking cannabis in the garden outside his house.'

The nose went up again. 'And did anyone arrest him for it? Of course they didn't.'

'This isn't a totalitarian state, we can't just—'

'Are you going to arrest him or not?'

'We need evidence before—'

She jabbed the desk with a finger. 'I *had* thought you might be different. That you'd be an *honest* policeman for a change, unlike the rest of these corrupt—'

'Now hold on, that's—'

'—clearly in the pocket of drug dealers and pornographers!'

Logan shuffled his chair back from the table an inch. 'Pornographers?'

'Justin Robson posted an obscene publication through my door; a magazine full of women performing the most revolting acts.' Her mouth puckered like a chicken's bum. A sniff. 'Mr Black had to burn it in the back garden. Well, it's not as if we could've put it in the recycling, what would the binmen think?'

'Mrs Black, I can assure you that neither I, nor any of my team are being paid off by drug dealers *or* pornographers. We can't arrest Mr Robson for smoking marijuana two years ago, because there's no evidence.'

She hissed a breath out through that long raised nose. 'I saw him with my own eyes!'

'I see.' Logan wrote that down in his notebook. 'And how did you determine that what he was smoking was actually marijuana? Did you perform a chemical analysis on the roach? Did you see him roll it?'

'Don't be facetious.'

'I'm not being facetious, I'm trying to understand why you think he was smoking—'

17

'You're not going to do anything about him putting dog mess on my cherry tree, are you? You're going to sit there and do nothing, because you're as corrupt as all the rest.'

Slow, calm breaths.

Logan opened the folder and pulled out the thick wad of paperwork. 'Mrs Black, in the last two years, you've made five hundred and seventeen complaints against Mr Robson; the local council; the Scottish Government; the Prince of Wales; Jimmy Shand; Ewan McGregor; the whole Westminster cabinet; our local MP, MSP, *and* MEP; and nearly every police officer in Aberdeen Division.'

'I have a moral obligation, and a *right*, to report corruption wherever I find it!'

'OK.' He reached beneath the desk and pulled a fresh complaint form from the bottom of the pile. Placed it in front of her. 'If you'd like to report me for taking money from drug dealers and pornographers, you should speak to someone from Professional Standards. I can give you their number.'

She curled her top lip. 'What makes you think they're not all corrupt too?'

Logan pushed through the double doors, out onto the rear-podium car park. The bulk of Divisional Headquarters formed walls of concrete and glass on three sides, the back of the next street over closing the gap, turning it into a sun trap. Which meant the pool car was like a sodding oven when he unlocked the door.

Then froze.

Scowled.

Leaned back against the bonnet and crossed his arms as a dented brown Vauxhall spluttered its way up the ramp and into the parking space opposite.

The driver gave Logan a smile and a wave as he climbed out into the sunshine. Broad face with ruddy cheeks, no neck, greying hair that wasn't as fond of his head as it had been twenty years ago. A proper farmer's face. 'Fine day, the day, Guv. Do—'

'Wheezy! Where the bloody hell have you been?'

DC Andrews's mouth clicked shut, then his eyebrows peaked in the middle. 'I've been taking witness—'

'I had to interview Marion Sodding Black!'

'It's not my fault, I wasn't even here!' He cleared his throat. Coughed. Covered his mouth and hacked out a couple of barks that ended with a glob of phlegm being spat against the tarmac. Leaving his ruddy farmer's face red and swollen. 'Gah...' Deep, groaning breaths.

Then Logan closed his eyes. Counted to three. Wheezy was right – it wasn't his fault he was out working when Mrs Black turned up. 'OK. I'm sorry. That was unfair.' He straightened his jacket. 'Did you find anything out at Garthdee?'

'Oh, aye.' Wheezy Doug locked his pool car. 'Fiver says it was Bobby Greig. Security camera's didn't get his face, but I'd recognize that manky BMX bike of his anywhere.'

'Good. That's good.' Logan went for an innocent smile. 'So you're free right now?'

'As I can be. Need to get a search warrant and...' Wheezy Doug pulled his chin in, giving himself a ripple of neck wrinkles. Narrowed his eyes. 'Wait a minute: *why*?'

'Oh, just asking.'

He backed off a pace. 'No you're not. You've got something horrible needs doing, don't you?'

'Me? No. Not a bit of it. I want you to go visit Pitmedden Court for me. Take a look at a cherry tree for me.'

Wheezy Doug's face unclenched. 'Oh, that's OK then. Thought for a moment there you...' And then it was back again. 'Pitmedden *Court*? Gah...' He covered his eyes with his hands. 'Noooooo ... It's her, isn't it?'

The innocent smile turned into a grin. 'Mrs Black says

her neighbour's sticking dog poo in her tree. And you're officially in possession of the Nutter Spoon of Doom.'

'Mrs Black's a pain in the hoop.'

'Yup, but right now she's *your* pain. Now get your hoop in gear and go check out her tree.'

Logan tucked his phone between his ear and his shoulder, then locked the pool car's door. 'Nah, same nonsense as usual. Everyone's corrupt. Everyone's out to get her. Her neighbour's hanging bags of dog crap in her cherry tree.'

On the other end, DS Baird groaned. *'Dog crap? I must've missed that issue of* Better Homes and Gardens. *Stoney's back – says are you coming to the pub after work?'*

Quick check of the watch: five to four.

'Depends how long I am here. Yeah. Well, probably.'

Wind rustled through the thick green crown of a sycamore tree, dropping helicopter seed pods onto the pool car's bonnet to lie amongst the dappled sunlight. Buchanan Street's grey terraces faced each other across a short stretch of divoted tarmac. Eight houses on each side in utilitarian granite, unadorned by anything fancier than UPVC windows and doors. Most of the gardens had been converted into off-street parking, bordered by knee-high walls and the occasional browning hedge.

Number Fourteen's parking area was empty, but a useless Police Constable and his patrol car idled outside – blocking the drive.

The house didn't look any different to its neighbours. As if nothing had happened. As if the guy who lived there hadn't jumped off the casino roof and splattered himself across Exchequer Row.

Logan hung up and wandered over to the patrol car. Knocked on the driver's window.

Sitting behind the wheel, PC Guthrie gave a little squeak and sat bolt upright, stuffing a magazine into the footwell before Logan could get a good look at it. He turned and hauled on a pained smile, pink blooming on his cheeks as he buzzed down the window. 'Sorry, Guv. Frightened the life out of me.'

Logan leaned on the roof of the car, looming through the open window. 'That better not have been porn, Sunshine, or I swear to God...'

The blush deepened. 'Porn? No. No, course not.' He cleared his throat then grabbed his hat and climbed out into the afternoon. 'I've been round all the neighbours: no one's seen Mrs Skinner since she took the kids to school this morning.'

Logan turned on the spot. Sixteen houses, all crushed together. 'It's Saturday, why was she taking the kids to school?'

'Ballet classes for the wee boy, and maths club for the girl. He's six, she's seven.'

Made sense. 'You tried the school?'

A shrug. 'Closes at two on a Saturday.'

Well, it wasn't as if they'd still be there anyway. Not now. 'OK. Any of the neighbours got a contact number for Mrs Skinner?'

Guthrie pulled out his notepad and flicked through to the marker. Passed it over. 'Mobile: goes straight to voicemail.'

Logan tried it anyway.

Click. 'Hello, this is Emma, I can't do the phone thing right now, so make messages after the bleep.' Beeeeeep.

'Mrs Skinner, this is Detective Inspector Logan McRae of Police Scotland. Can you give me a call when you get this, please? You can get back to me on this number, or call one-zero-one and ask them to put you through. Thanks.' He hung up. Put his phone away.

Guthrie sniffed, then slid the back of a finger underneath his nose, as if trying to catch a drip. 'Shame we can't deliver the death message by text, isn't it?'

Logan stared at him, until the blush came back. 'For that

21

little moment of compassion, you can stay here till she comes home.'

His shoulders dipped. 'Guv.'

'And stop reading porn in the patrol car!'

Logan pulled in to the kerb and swore his mobile phone out of his pocket. Checked the display. No idea who the number belonged to. Might be Mrs Skinner calling back?

He hit the button. 'DI McRae.'

Harlaw playing fields lay flat and green behind their high wire fence. Three cricket matches, and a game of rugby, grunting and thwacking away in the afternoon light.

Logan tried again. 'Hello?'

A familiar dark, clipped female voice sounded in his ear: *'You were supposed to be investigating my tree.'*

'Mrs Black.' Oh joy.

'I'll be putting in a formal complaint. I know my rights! You have to—'

'We *are* investigating, Mrs Black.' Keep it calm and level. No shouting. No swearing or telling her what she can do with her sodding complaints. Don't sigh. 'I've sent an officer round there. He will be taking statements. He will be photographing any evidence. OK?' You vile, rancid, old battle-axe.

Silence.

Outside, a scruffy man with a beard down to the middle of his chest and hair like a diseased scarecrow lurched along the pavement. Scruffy overcoat, suit trousers, hiking boots, trilby hat. Not the best fashion statement in the world.

A carrier bag swung from one hand, like a pendulum. Something heavy in there. And from the look of him, it was probably cheap and very alcoholic.

Then Mrs Black was back. *'That* man *is making my life a living hell and you're doing nothing to prevent it. What about my human rights? I demand you* do *something!'*

22

Seriously?

Deep breath. 'We are doing something. We're *investigating*.' Logan coiled his other hand around the steering wheel. Strangling it. 'Mrs Black, if Mr Robson's done something illegal under Scottish law, we'll arrest him. Putting dog mess in someone's tree is antisocial, but it isn't illegal.'

'Of course it's illegal! How could it not be illegal?' She was getting louder and shriller. *'I can't sleep, I can't breathe, I can't … Mr Black…'* A deep breath. *'It's the law. He's harassing me. He's putting dog mess in my cherry tree!'*

Captain Scruffy stumbled into the path of a large woman wheeling a pushchair along the pavement.

She flinched to a halt, detoured around him. Shuddering as she marched off.

He wobbled in place, plastic bag clutched to his chest, yelling slurred obscenities after her.

'I demand you arrest that Robson creature!'

'Mrs Black, this is a *civil* matter, not a criminal one. You need to get yourself a lawyer and sue him.'

'Why should I spend all that money on a lawyer, when it's your job to arrest him? I demand you do your job!'

Captain Scruffy shook his fist at the escaping woman. The motion sent him off again: one step to the right. One to the left. Two to the right. And on his backside in three, two…

'Are you even listening to me?'

The next stagger took him backwards, off the kerb and into the traffic.

Sodding hell.

A blare of horns. An Audi estate swerved, barely missing him with its front bumper. A Range Rover slammed on its brakes.

Captain Scruffy pirouetted, carrier bag swinging out with the motion.

BANG. A bright-orange Mini caught the bag, right on the

23

bonnet, spinning him around and bouncing him off the windscreen. Sending him clattering to the tarmac like a bag of dirty laundry.

'Why won't anyone there take me seriously? I pay my taxes! I have rights! How dare *you ignore me!'*

Logan clicked off his seatbelt.

'I have to go.'

'Don't you dare hang up on me, I—'

He hung up on her and scrambled out into the warm afternoon.

The Mini was slewed at thirty degrees across both lanes, its driver already out of the car staring at the bonnet. 'Oh God, oh God, oh God…' She had a hand to her mouth, eyes wide, knees trembling. Didn't seem to be even vaguely interested in the man lying on his back in the middle of the road behind her.

Then she turned on him. 'YOU BLOODY IDIOT! WHAT'S MUM GOING TO SAY?' Two fast steps, then she slammed a trainer into the fallen man's stomach. 'SHE'S ONLY HAD IT A WEEK!' Another kick, this one catching him on the side of the head, sending that stupid little hat flying.

The other drivers stayed where they were, in their cars. No one helped, but a couple dragged out their mobile phones to film it, so that was all right.

Logan ran. Grabbed her by the arm and spun her around. 'That's enough!'

She swung a fist at Logan's head. So he slammed her into the side of her mum's car, grabbed her wrist and put it into a lock hold. Applying pressure till her legs buckled. 'AAAAAAAAGH! Get off me! GET OFF ME! RAPE! RAPE! HELP!'

He pulled his cuffs out. 'I'm detaining you under Section Fourteen of the Criminal Procedure – Scotland – Act 1995, because I suspect you of having committed an offence punishable by imprisonment—'

'RAPE! HELP! SOMEONE HELP ME! RAPE!'

24

No one got out of their car.

'You are not obliged to say anything, but anything you do say—'

'HELP! HELP!'

Deep breath: 'WOULD YOU SHUT UP?'

She went limp. Slumped forward until her forehead was resting on the new Mini's roof. 'It's only a week old. She'll never let me borrow it again.'

Logan clicked the cuffs over her wrists. 'But anything you do say will be noted down and may be used in evidence.' Then steered her over to the pool car and stuffed her into the back. 'Stay there. Don't make it any worse.'

He got out his phone again and dialled Control. 'I need an ambulance to Cromwell Road, got an … Hold on.'

Captain Scruffy had levered himself up onto his bum, wobbling there with blood pouring down his filthy face. Eyes bloodshot and blinking out of phase with one another.

Logan squatted down in front of him. 'Are you OK?'

An aura of rotting vegetables, BO, and baked-on urine spread out like a fog.

It took a bit, but eventually that big hairy head swung around to squint at him. 'Broke my bottle…' He clutched the carrier bag to his chest. Bits of broken glass stuck out through the plastic. 'BROKE MY BOTTLE!' The bottom lip trembled, then tears sparked up in those pinky-yellow eyes, tumbled down the filthy cheeks. 'NOOOOOOOO!'

'You're a bloody idiot, you know that, don't you?' Back to the phone. 'We've got an IC-One male who's been hit by a car and assaulted.' Logan nodded at him, trying not to breathe through his nose. 'What's your name?'

'My bottle … My lovely, lovely, bottle.' He hauled in air, showing off a mouth full of twisted brown teeth. 'BASTARDS! *MY* BOTTLE!'

Yeah, it was definitely one of those days.

25

4

'Logan, we don't normally see you here during the day.' Claire stuck her book down on the nurses' station desk and smiled at him, making two dimples in her smooth round cheeks. 'To what do we owe the honour?'

Logan pointed over his shoulder, back along the corridor. 'Got a road-rage victim in A-and-E. Thought I'd pop past while they were stitching him up.'

Claire squeezed one eye shut. 'It's not a hairy young gentleman with personal hygiene issues, is it? Only Donald from security was just in here moaning about being bitten.'

Yeah, probably. 'How's Samantha today?'

'Getting up to all sorts of hijinks.' She stood and smoothed out the creases in her nurse's scrubs. 'You got time for a cup of tea?'

'Wouldn't say no.'

'Oh, and this came for you this morning.' Claire reached into a drawer and pulled out a grey envelope. 'Think it's from Sunny Glen.'

'Thanks.' He took it and wandered down the corridor to Samantha's room.

The blinds were drawn, shutting out most of the light, but it was still warm enough to make him yawn.

He sank onto the edge of the bed, leaned in and gave her a kiss on the cheek. Cold and pale. 'Hey, you.'

She didn't answer, but then she never did.

Something about the gloom and her porcelain skin made the tattoos stand out even more than usual. Jagged and dark. Like something trying to crawl its way out of her body.

He brushed a strand of brown hair from her face. 'Got a reply from Sunny Glen.' Logan held up the envelope. 'What do you think?'

No reply.

'Yeah, me too.' He ripped it open. '"Dear Mr McRae, thank you for the application for specialist residential care on behalf of your girlfriend Samantha Mackie. As you know, our Neurological Care Unit has a worldwide reputation for managing and treating those in long-term comas..." Blah, blah, blah.' He turned the letter over. 'Oh sodding hell. "Unfortunately we do not have any spaces available at the current time." Could they not have said that in the first place?' He crumpled the sheet of paper into a ball and lobbed it across the room at the bin. Missed. Slouched over and put it in properly. 'Place is probably rubbish anyway. And it's all the way up on the sodding coast, not exactly convenient, is it? Traipsing all the way up there. You'd have hated it.'

Still felt as if someone had used his soul as cat litter, though.

'Doesn't matter. We've got another three applications out there. Bound to be one who'll take a hell-raiser like you.'

Nothing.

A knock on the door, and Claire stuck her head into the room. 'I even managed to find a couple of biscuits for you. So...' She frowned as Logan's phone launched into its

27

anonymous ringtone. 'How many times do we have to talk about this?'

'Only be a minute.' He pulled it out and hit the button. 'McRae.'

A man's voice, sounding out of breath. *'You the joker who brought in Gordon Taylor?'*

Who the hell was Gordon Taylor? 'Sorry?'

'The homeless guy – got hit by a car. Someone gave him a kicking.'

Ah, right. *That* Gordon Taylor. 'What about him?'

'He's bitten two security guards and punched a nurse.'

Wonderful. Another dollop added to the cat litter. 'I'll be right down.' He put his phone away. Took the mug of tea from Claire and kissed her on the cheek. 'Don't let Samantha give you any trouble, OK? You know how feisty she gets.'

The elevator juddered to a halt, and Logan stepped out into the familiar, depressing, scuffed green corridors. No paintings on the walls here, no community art projects, or murals, or anything to break the bleak industrial gloom. He followed the coloured lines set into the floor.

Here and there, squares of duct tape held the peeling surface together. And everything smelled of disinfectant and over-boiled cauliflower.

A porter bustled past, pushing a small child in a big bed. Drips and tubes and wires snaking from the little body to various bags and bits of equipment.

Logan pulled out his phone and called Guthrie. 'Any sign of Mrs Skinner yet?'

'Sorry, Guv. I've checked all the neighbours again, but no one's heard from her.'

'OK.' He stepped around the corner, and stopped outside the doors to Accident and Emergency. 'Get onto Control and see if you can…' A frown. 'Have you been round the house? Peered in all the windows? Just in case.'

'Yup. Even got her next-door to let me through so I could climb the garden fence and have a squint in the back. She's not lying dead on the floor anywhere.'

At least that was something.

'Get Control to dig up the grandparents. They might know where she is.'

'Will do.' A pause. *'Guv, did I ever tell you about what happened last time Snow White—'*

'Yes. And *no more* porn in the patrol car.'

Logan hung up, pushed the door open, and stepped inside.

It wasn't difficult to find Gordon Taylor, not with all the shouting and swearing going on. He was in a cubicle at the far end – *crash, bang, wallop*. A nurse squatted outside the curtains, head thrown back, a wad of tissues clamped against her nose stained bright red.

'Hold still, you little sod…'

'Ow!'

'Can someone hold his head so he won't bite?'

'Ow! Ow, ow, ow … Bloody hell…'

Logan slipped through the curtains and stared at the human octopus wrestling with itself on the hospital bed. Arms, legs, hands, feet, all struggling to keep the figure on the bottom from getting up.

One of the nurses yanked her arm into the air. 'OW! He bit me!'

'Don't let go of his head!'

Logan reached into his pocket, pulled out the little canister of CS gas, and walked over to the bed. 'Let go of him.'

A doctor turned and glared. 'Are you off your head?'

Click, the safety cover flipped off the top of the gas canister. 'Then you probably want to cover your nose and mouth.'

Gordon Taylor's filthy, blood-caked face rose from between the medics' arms, teeth snapping.

Logan jammed the CS gas canister right between his eyes.

29

Raised his voice over the crashing and banging, the grunting and swearing. 'You've been gassed before, right, Gordon? Want to try it again?'

A blink. Then he froze.

'Good boy. Now you let these nice people examine you, or I'm going to gas you back to the Thatcher era, OK?'

Gordon Taylor went limp.

The doctor bowed his head for a moment. 'Oh thank God...' Then straightened up. 'Right, we need blood tests and a sedative. Then get these filthy rags off him.'

The nurses bustled about with needles and scissors, faces contorted with disgust every time a new layer of clothes came off revealing a new odour.

Logan kept the CS gas where Taylor could see it. 'You're an idiot, you know that, don't you? Staggering about, blootered, abusing passers-by, falling into the road. Lucky you didn't kill yourself.'

Taylor didn't move. Kept his eyes fixed on the gas canister.

One of the nurses gagged, holding out a filthy shirt with her fingertips.

Gordon Taylor's arms were knots of ropey muscles, stretched taut across too-big bones. No fat on them. But the left one had a Gordon Highlanders tattoo, the ink barely visible beneath the filth. His torso was a mess of bruises – some fresh and red, some middle-aged purple-and-blue, some dying yellow-and-green.

He jerked his chin up. 'She broke my bottle.' The slur had gone from his voice, but his breath was enough to make Logan back off a couple of steps.

'You're a drunken sodding menace to yourself and others, Gordon. What the hell were you thinking, staggering out into the road? What if a car swerves, trying to avoid your drunken backside, hits someone else and kills them? That what you want?'

'A whole bottle of Bells that was!' No wonder his breath was minging – his teeth looked like stubbed-out cigarettes.

'I've arrested the woman who assaulted you. She'll—'

'Tell her! Tell her I'll not press charges if she buys me a new bottle...' Gordon Taylor's eyes widened. 'No, *two* bottles. Aye, and litre bottles, not tiny wee ones.'

Nothing like getting your priorities straight.

'That's not how it works, Gordon. She has to—' Logan's phone burst into song in his pocket. 'Sodding hell.'

The doctor narrowed his eyes. 'You're not supposed to have your phone switched on in here.'

'Police business.' He pulled it out and hit the button, killing the noise. 'For God's sake, what *now*?'

There was a moment of silence, then a deep voice rumbled out of the speakers. *'I think you mean, "Good afternoon", don't you, Acting Detective Inspector McRae?'*

Oh no. Not this. Not now.

Logan closed his eyes. 'Superintendent Young. Sorry. I'm kind of in the middle of—'

'I think you and I need to have a chat about a complaint that's landed on my desk. Why don't we say, my office? Any time in the next fifteen minutes is good.'

Wonderful.

5

Superintendent Young was all dressed up in Nosferatu black – black T-shirt with epaulettes, black police-issue trousers, and black shoes. He sat back in his seat and tapped his pen against an A4 pad. Tap. Tap. Tap. 'Are you denying the allegations?'

The Professional Standards office was tombstone quiet. A wooden clock ticked away to itself on the wall beside Young's desk. The chair creaked beneath Logan's bum. A muffled scuffing sound as someone tried to sneak past outside – scared to make a noise in case someone inside heard them and came hunting. And the sinister sods didn't burst into flame when exposed to sunlight *or* holy water, so you were never safe.

Trophies made a little gilded plastic parade across the two filing cabinets in the corner, all the figures frozen in the execution of their chosen sport – clay-pigeon shooting, judo, boxing, ten-pin bowling, fly-fishing, curling. A framed print of *The Monarch of the Glen* above the printer.

Tick. Tick. Tick.

Quarter past five. Should be in the pub by now, not sitting here.

Logan dumped the letter of complaint back on Young's desk. 'With all due respect to anyone unfortunate enough to suffer from mental illness, Marion Black is a complete and utter sodding nutter.'

'You didn't answer my question.'

Logan shifted in the creaky chair. 'While I do *know* a pornographer, he's never offered me a bribe.'

Young raised an eyebrow. 'You actually know someone who makes dirty movies?'

'Helps us out from time to time cleaning up CCTV footage. Moved into mainstream film a couple of years ago. Ever see *Witchfire*? That was him.'

'And he used to make porn?'

'You should ask DCI Steel to show you – she's got the complete collection.'

A tilt of the head, as if Young was considering doing just that. 'What about drug dealers?'

'Guv, Marion Black has accused nearly everyone in a three hundred mile radius of corruption at some point. She's a menace. You *know* that.'

'It doesn't matter how many complaints an individual makes, Logan, we have to take every one of them seriously.'

Logan poked the letter. It was a printout from a slightly blotchy inkjet, the words on the far left of the pages smudged. Densely packed type with no line breaks. 'I met her at ten past three today, and spoke to her on the phone a little after four. And in that time she managed to write a three-page letter of complaint and deliver it to you lot. She's probably got a dozen of them sitting on her computer ready to go at any time. Insert-some-poor-sod's-name-here and off you go.'

Young swivelled his chair from side to side a couple of times. 'It's not going to work, you know.'

'What isn't?'

'This.' Young spread his hands, taking in the whole room. 'You think the easiest way to get shot of Mrs Black is to ignore her. You do nothing about her concerns, she makes a complaint

33

about corruption, and you get to pass the Nutter Spoon of Doom on to the next poor sod without having to do any work.'

Warmth prickled at the back of Logan's neck. He licked his lips. 'Nutter Spoon of Doom, Guv? I don't think I've ever heard of—'

'Oh don't be ridiculous, we know all about it.' He sat forward. 'Let me make this abundantly clear, *Acting* Detective Inspector McRae: you have the spoon, and you're going to personally deal with Mrs Black whether you like it or not.' A finger came up, pointing at the middle of Logan's chest. 'Not one of your minions: you.'

Logan threw his arms out, appealing to the ref. 'I met her today at three o'clock! I've got a suicide, a road-rage incident, a spate of car vandalism, petty thefts, fire-raising, a shoplifting ring, three common assaults, and a bunch of other cases to deal with. When was I supposed to go visit her poo tree?'

'*Make* time.'

'I delegated the task to DC Andrews.'

'I don't care.' Young sat back again. 'And make sure you never speak to Mrs Black without another officer present. Preferably someone who can film it on their body-worn video.'

Logan stared at the ceiling tiles for a moment. They were clean. New and pristine. 'I'm not even supposed to be holding the spoon – it's Wheezy Doug's turn.'

'My heart bleeds.' Superintendent Young prodded the complaint file. 'What about this man Mrs Black complained about in the first place…?'

'Justin Robson. She claims to have seen him smoking cannabis in his garden two and a bit years ago. Says he's now festooning her cherry tree with what she calls "dog mess".'

'I see.' Young narrowed his eyes, tapped his fingertips against his pursed lips. 'And how has CID investigated this unwelcomed act of garden embellishment?'

Logan shrugged. 'I told Wheezy Doug to go take a look this afternoon. Haven't had time to catch up with him yet.'

'Hmm...'

Silence.

Young pursed and tapped.

Logan just sat there.

Tick. Tick. Tick.

More pursing and tapping. Then: 'I think it's about time someone looked into Mrs Black's neighbour. I want you to have a word with this Justin Robson. Ask him, politely, to defuse his feud with Mrs Black. And tell him to *stop* decorating her tree with dog shit. Or at least wait until Christmas. It's only August.'

Wonderful. Makework. As if they didn't have enough to do.

'Guv, with all due respect, it—'

'Get cracking this evening; I'll authorize the overtime. Let's see if we can't at least *look* like we're taking her seriously.'

'Sorry, Guv, still no sign of Mrs Skinner or the kids.' Guthrie sniffed down the phone. *'You want me to hang on some more?'*

'Does she have her own car?' Logan unbuckled his seatbelt, as DC Wheezy Doug Andrews parked the pool car behind a Volvo Estate.

Pitmedden Court basked in the evening light. A long collection of grey harled houses, some in terraces of three or four, some semidetatched. Some with tiny portico porches, some without. A nice road. Tidy gardens and knee-high garden walls. Speed bumps. Hello, Mrs McGillivray, I hope your Jack's doing well the day.

'Hold on ... Yes: dark-green Honda Jazz.'

'Get a lookout request on the go. And make sure the Automatic Number Plate Recognition lot are keeping an eye out. Enough people filmed her husband jumping off the roof on their phones; I don't want the poor woman seeing him splattered across the cobbles on the evening news.'

'Guv.'

'What about the grandparents?'

'Got an address in Portlethen, and one in Stoneywood. You want me to pack it in here and go speak to them? Or hang about in case she comes home?'

Logan checked his watch: five past six. 'Abandon ship. Better give his parents the death message first, then see if either set knows where she is. And get on to the media office too – we need a blanket ban on anything that can ID John Skinner till we've spoken to the wife.' Logan put his phone back in his pocket. Turned to Wheezy Doug. 'We ready?'

His bottom lip protruded an inch as he tugged the fluorescent yellow high-viz waistcoat on over his suit jacket. 'Feel like a right neep.'

'It's what all the stylish young men about town are wearing this season. And if you'd looked into it when I sodding well *told* you to, we wouldn't be here now.'

A blush darkened Wheezy's cheeks. 'Sorry, Guv.' He fiddled a BWV unit onto one of the clips that pimpled the waistcoat's front, like nipples on a cat. The body-worn video unit was about the same size and shape as a packet of cigarettes; with a white credit-card style front with the Police Scotland logo, a camera icon, and the words 'CCTV In Operation' on it. 'Don't see why you couldn't have got some spod from Uniform to do this bit, though.'

'Because she's filed *complaints* against all the spods from Uniform. No more whingeing.' Logan climbed out into the sunshine. 'Come on.'

The street's twin rows of tidy gardens were alive with the sound of lawns being mowed. Gravel being raked. Cars being washed. The screech and yell of little children playing. The bark of an overexcited dog. The smell of charcoal and grilling meat oozing its way in through the warm August air.

Wheezy Doug sighed, then joined him. Pulled out the keys and plipped the pool car's locks. 'That's the one over there – wishing well, crappy cherry tree, and leylandii hedge.'

The hedge was a proper spite job: at least eight-foot-tall, casting thick dark shadows across the neighbouring property's lawn.

Logan puffed out a breath. 'Suppose we'd better do this.' He marched across the road to the garden gate. Stopped and looked up at the cherry tree.

It was thick with shining green leaves, the swelling fruits drooping on wishbone stalks. And tied onto nearly every branch was a small blue plastic bag with something heavy and dark in it. There had to be at least twenty of them on there. Maybe thirty?

Young was right – it did look … inappropriately festive.

'Right. First up, Justin Robson.' Logan walked along the front wall, past the thicket of spiteful hedge, and in through the gate next door. All nice and tidy, with rosebushes in lustrous shades of red-and-gold, and a sundial lawn ornament that was two hours out.

Honeysuckle grew up one side of the front door and over the lintel, hanging with searing yellow flowers. Scenting the air.

Wheezy Doug stifled a cough. 'Doesn't really look like a drug den, does it?' Then turned and nodded at the white BMW parked out front: spoiler, alloys, low-profile tyres. 'The *car*, on the other hand has Drug Dealer written all over it.' A howch and a spit. He wiped the line of spittle from his chin. 'Right, everyone on their best behaviour, it's Candid Camera time.' He slid the white credit-card cover down, setting the body-worn video recording. Cleared his throat. 'Detective Constable Douglas Andrews, twentieth August, at thirteen Pitmedden Court, Kincorth, Aberdeen. Present is DI McRae.' A nod. 'OK, Guv.'

Logan got as far as the first knock when the door swung open.

A short man with trendy hair and a stripy apron stared up at them through smeared glasses. 'Yes?'

He held up his warrant card. 'Detective Inspector McRae, CID. Are you Justin Robson?'

'That was quick, I only called two minutes ago.' He stepped back, wiping his hands on the green-and-white stripes, leaving dark-red smears.

OK … That *definitely* looked like blood.

'Mr Robson?' Logan's right hand drifted inside his jacket, where the small canister of CS gas lurked. 'Is everything OK, sir?'

'No it's not. Not by a long sodding chalk.' Then he blinked a couple of times. 'Sorry, where are my manners, come in, come in.' Reversing down the hallway and into the kitchen.

Wheezy Doug's voice dropped to a whisper, a wee smile playing at the corners of his mouth. 'Was that blood? Maybe he's killed Mrs Black and hacked her up?'

They should be so lucky.

Logan gave it a beat, then followed Robson through into the kitchen.

It was compact, but kitted out with a fancy-looking oven and induction hob. Built-in deep-fat fryer, American-style double fridge freezer. A glass of white wine sat on the granite countertop, next to two racks of ribs on a chopping board.

Wheezy Doug reached for his cuffs as Robson reached for a cleaver. Pointed. 'Oh no you don't. Put the knife down and—'

'Knife…? Oh, this.' He wiggled it a couple of times. 'Sorry, but we've got friends coming round and I need to get these ready.' The cleaver's shiny blade slipped between the rib bones, slicing through flesh and cartilage as if they were yoghurt. 'I hope you're going to arrest her.'

38

Nope, no idea.

Logan let go of his CS gas. 'Perhaps you should start from the beginning, sir? Make sure nothing's got lost in translation.'

'That…' the cleaver thumped through the next chunk of flesh, '*bitch* next door. I mean, look at them!' He pointed the severed bone at a small pile of crumpled A4 sheets on the kitchen table. 'That's slander. It's illegal. I know my rights.'

Not another one.

Wheezy Doug picked a sheet from the top of the pile. Pulled a face. 'Actually, sir, slander would be if she *said* this to someone, once it's in writing it's libel.' He handed the bit of paper to Logan.

A black-and-white photo of Justin Robson sat beneath the words, 'GET THIS DRUG DEALING SCUM OFF OUR STREETS!!!'

Ah…

Logan scanned the paragraph at the bottom of the page:

This so-called "man" is **DEALING DRUGS** in Kincorth! He does it from his home and various establishments around town. How will *YOU* feel when he starts selling them outside the school gates where *YOUR* child goes to learn? Our **CORRUPTION-RIDDEN** police force do nothing while *HE* corrupts our children with **POISON**!

Robson hacked off another rib. 'I mean, for God's sake, it's got my photo and my home address and my telephone number on it. And they're all over the place!' Hack, thump, hack. 'I want that woman locked up, she's a bloody menace.'

'I see.' Logan took another look around the room. Wheezy Doug was right, it didn't really look like a drug dealer's house. Far too clean for that. Still, belt and braces: 'And *are* you selling drugs to schoolchildren, Mr Robson?'

'This isn't *Breaking Bad*.' Hack. Thump. Hack. 'I don't deal drugs, I programme distributed integration applications for the oil industry. That's quite enough excitement for me.' He pulled over the second rack of ribs. 'You can search the place, if you like? If it'll finally shut *her* up.'

A nod. 'We might take you up on that.' Logan folded the notice and slipped it into a jacket pocket. 'Mr Robson, Mrs Black tells me that you've been putting "dog mess" in her cherry tree. Is that true? We checked, and the thing's covered in poop-scoop bags.'

Hack, hack, hack. 'I don't have a dog. Does this look like a house that has a dog? Nasty, smelly, dirty things.'

'I didn't ask if you *had* a dog, Mr Robson, I asked if you were responsible for putting … dog waste in her tree.'

He stopped hacking and stared, face wrinkled on one side. 'Are you seriously suggesting that I prowl the streets of Aberdeen, collecting other people's dog shit, just so I can put it in her tree? Really?' Hack. Thump. Hack.

'Everyone needs a hobby.'

'Trust me, I've got better things to do with my spare time.' The second rack of ribs ended up a lot less neat than the first. He dumped them all in a big glass bowl. 'All she ever does is cause trouble. Like she's so perfect, with her screaming and crying at all hours of the night. Her and her creepy husband. And her bloody, sodding…' A deep breath, then Robson slopped in some sort of sauce from a jug. Dug his hands in and mixed the whole lot up. Squeezing the ribs like he was strangling them. 'Have you ever had to live next door to three hundred thousand nasty little parakeets? Squawking and screeching and flapping at all hours. Not to mention the *smell*. And will the council do anything about it? No, of course they sodding won't.'

He thumped over to the sink and washed his hands. 'I swear to God, one of these days—'

'Actually,' Logan held up a hand, 'it might be an idea to remember there's two police officers in the room before you go making death threats.'

Robson's head slumped. Then he dried his hands. 'I'm sorry. It's … that woman drives me *insane*.' He opened the back door and took his bowl of glistening bones and meat out onto a small decking area, where a kettle barbecue sat. The rich earthy scent of wood-smoke embraced them, not quite covering the bitter ammonia stink coming from the other side of another massive leylandii hedge that blotted out the light.

Squeaking and chirping prickled the air, partially muffled by the dense green foliage.

Wheezy Doug stared up at the hedge. Sniffed. Then clicked the cover up on his body-worn video, stopping it recording. 'You know, I remember this one terrace where … well, let's call them "Couple A" put up a huge hedge to spite "Couple B". So "Couple B" snuck out in the middle of the night and watered it with tree-stump killer for a fortnight. Not that Police Scotland would advocate such behaviour. Would we, Guv?'

'Don't worry.' Robson creaked up the lid of the barbecue and put down a double layer of tinfoil on the bars. 'That hedge is the only thing between me and those revolting birds, there's no way I'm sabotaging it.' He laid out the ribs in careful bony rows.

Logan nodded back at the house. 'Sorry to be a pain, but can I use your toilet?'

'Top of the stairs.' More ribs joined their comrades.

'Won't be a minute.'

Back through the kitchen and into the hall. Quick left turn into the lounge.

Well, Robson did say they could search the place if they liked. Fancy patterned wallpaper made up a single swirly green-and-black graphic across one wall. A huge flatscreen television was hooked up to a PlayStation, an X-Box, and what looked like a very expensive surround sound system. Black leather couch. All spotless.

Cupboard under the stairs: hoover, ironing board, shelves with cleaning products arranged in neat rows.

Upstairs.

The master bedroom had a king-sized bed against one wall, with a black duvet cover and too many pillows. Both bedside cabinets were topped with a lamp and a clock radio. No clutter. The clothes in the wardrobe arranged by colour.

The spare room was kitted out as a study. Shelves covered one wall, stuffed with programming manuals and reference books. Fancy desk, big full-colour laser printer, ergonomic chair. Framed qualification certificates above a beige filing cabinet.

Two big speakers rested against the adjoining wall, with their backs to the room and their fronts against the plaster-board. Both were wired into an amplifier with an iPod plugged into the top. The perfect setup for blasting rap music through the bricks at your neighbours in the dead of night.

So Justin Robson wasn't exactly the put-upon innocent he pretended to be.

A quick check of the linen cupboard – just to be thorough – then through to the bathroom for a rummage in the medicine cabinet. Nothing out of the ordinary. Well, except for two packs of antidepressants, but they had chemist's stickers on the outside with dosage instructions, Robson's name, and the prescribing doctor's details. All aboveboard.

Might as well play out the charade properly.

Logan flushed the toilet, unused, and washed his hands. Headed back downstairs.

'Well, thank you for your time, Mr Robson. In case you're wondering: we'll be keeping an eye on Mrs Black's tree from now on. I'd appreciate it if you'd help us make sure there are no more decorations on there.'

Next door, Wheezy Doug leaned on the doorbell. 'What do you think? Is Robson our Phantom Pooper Scooper? The Defecation Decorator. The…' A frown. 'Christmas Tree Crapper?'

'Hmmm…' Logan turned towards the thick barrier of leylandii hedge – tall enough and thick enough to completely blot out all view of Justin Robson's house. 'He's a neat freak – the whole place is like a show home. Is someone that anal going to collect other people's dog shit to spite their neighbour? Don't know.' Stranger things had happened. And then there were those two heavy-duty speakers up against the wall in the study … 'Possibly.'

Mrs Black's garden wasn't nearly as tidy as her neighbour's. Dandelions and clover encroached on the lawn. More weeds in the borders. The cherry tree with its droopy blue plastic decorations.

Even if you removed every single one of them, would you *really* want to eat the fruit that had grown between those dangling bags?

Wheezy Doug sniffed, then stifled a cough. 'Can't really blame him though, can you? Living next to the Wicked Twit of the West would drive anyone barmy.' Another go on the bell. 'Maybe she's not in?'

'One more try, and we're off.' Superintendent Young could moan all he liked, they'd done their bit. Wasn't their fault Mrs Black was out.

The *drrrrrrrringgggg* sounded again as Wheezy ground his thumb against the button.

Then, finally, a silhouette appeared in the rippled glass panels that took up the top half of the door. A thin wobbly voice: 'Who is it?'

Logan poked Wheezy. 'You filming this?'

A quick fiddle with the BWV. 'Am now.'

'Good.' Logan leaned in close to the glass. 'Mrs Black? It's the police. Can you open up, please?'

She didn't move.

'Mrs Black?'

'It's not convenient.'

'We need to talk to you about a complaint.'

A breeze stirred the blue plastic poo bags, making them swing like filthy pendulums.

'Mrs Black?'

There was a *click* and the door pulled open a couple of inches.

She peered out at them, her short grey hair flat on one side, crusts of yellow clinging to the corners of her baggy eyes. A flash of tartan pyjamas. 'Have you arrested him yet?'

'Mrs Black, have you been putting these up around town?' Logan reached into his pocket and pulled out the folded flyer. Held it up so she could see it.

She stiffened. Her nose came up, and all trace of tremor in her voice was gone. 'The people here have a right to know.'

'If you have proof that Mr Robson is dealing drugs, why didn't you call us?'

'He's a vile, revolting individual. He should be … should be *castrated* and locked up where he can't hurt anyone any more.'

Logan put the flyer back in his pocket. Closed his eyes and counted to three. 'Mrs Black, you can't go making accusations like that without proof: it's libellous. And Mr Robson's made a formal complaint.'

Her face hardened. 'I should have known…'

'Mrs Black, can we come in please?'

'I've been complaining about him for *years* and did you do anything about it?' She bared her teeth. 'But as soon as

44

he says anything, you're over here with your jackboots and your threats!'

Don't sigh.

'No one's threatening you, Mrs Black. Do you have any proof that Mr Robson is dealing drugs?'

Her finger jabbed over Logan's shoulder. 'HE PUT DOG MESS IN MY TREE!'

'Do you have any proof? If you have proof we'll look at it and—'

'HE DESERVES TO DIE FOR WHAT HE'S PUT ME THROUGH!'

Wheezy Doug stepped forward, palms out. 'Mrs Black, I need you to calm down, OK?'

'HE'S SCUM!' Her voice dropped to a hissing whisper. 'Sitting in there with his drugs and his pornography and his filthy rap music. I *demand* you arrest him.'

The sound of whirring lawn mowers. A child somewhere singing about popping caps in some gangbanger's ass. A motorbike purring past on the road. All as Mrs Black stood there, trembling in her pyjamas, lips flecked with spittle.

Logan kept his voice low and neutral. 'I need you to stop putting up these posters. And if you *have* any evidence that Mr Robson is dealing drugs, I want you to call me.' He pulled out a Police Scotland business card with the station number on it. Held it out.

She stared at the card in his hand. Curled her lip. Spat at her feet. 'You're all as corrupt as each other.'

Then stepped back and slammed the door.

Not the result they'd hoped for, but no one could say they hadn't tried.

'So...' Wheezy Doug dragged the toe of his shoe along the path. 'Pub?'

Logan popped the business card through the letterbox. 'Pub.'

6

Sodding keyhole wouldn't hold still … The key skittered around the moving target, until finally it clicked into place.

Hurrah.

Logan picked up his fish supper again, and pushed through into the flat. Floor was a bit shifty too.

Deep breath.

He eased the door closed and shushed the Yale lock as it clunked shut. Wouldn't do to wake the neighbours. They wouldn't like that. Got to be a good neighbour. 'Shhhh…'

Then he dumped his keys on the little table by the radiator. 'Cthulhu? Daddy's home.'

Silence.

Little sod.

Logan grabbed the salt, vinegar, mayonnaise, and a tin of Stella from the kitchen and escorted his supper through into the pristine living room.

Whole place was unnaturally tidy, everything superfluous hidden away in various cupboards and the loft, leaving nothing behind but estate-agent approved set dressing. Like the two glossy magazines lined up perfectly with the edge of the coffee table. Or the line of candles on the windowsill.

The photos in the wooden frames lined up where the books used to be. Everything dusted and hoovered with OCD fervour. All so some pair of picky sods could take a quick sniff around then decide the flat wasn't 'big enough for them'. Scumbags.

He slumped into the couch then clicked the ring-pull off the Stella. Gulped down a mouthful. Stifled a burp.

Why? Who the hell was going to complain about it?

He took another swig, then let his diaphragm rattle.

Better.

The batter was a bit thick, but the fish was moist and meaty. The chips limp in a way that only chip shops could get away with. How come a chip shop couldn't get chips crispy? You'd think they'd be chip experts. Clue's in the name.

The light on the answering machine winked at him, like a malevolent rat with one glowing red eye.

He stuck two fingers up at it and went back to his flaccid chips.

Cthulhu finally deigned to put in an appearance, padding in on silent fuzzy feet, tail held high. All grey and brown and black and stripy, with a huge white ruff and little white paws. She popped up onto the arm of the couch, then sat there, blinking slowly at him.

'Oh, you love me when there's food in it for you, don't you?' But he blinked back and gave her a nugget of haddock anyway.

Cue purring and chewing.

And still the answering machine glowered with its ratty eye.

Tough. Whatever it was, it could wait till morning.

Fish for Logan. Fish for Cthulhu.

The answering machine didn't care.

He stuffed down a mouthful of chips, followed by a swig of Stella.

It kept on glowering.

'Oh for God's sake.' He levered himself to his feet and lurched across the rolling deck. Propped himself up with one hand on the shelf. Pressed the button.

'You have three new messages. Message one:' Bleeeeeep.

'Logan? It's your mother. Why do I always—'

'Gah!' He poked the machine.

'Message deleted. Message two:' Bleeeeeep.

'Hello? Mr McRae? It's Marjory from Willkie and Oxford, Solicitors. I know Mr and Mrs Moore said they weren't interested, but they've come back with an offer for the flat. It's twenty thousand less than the valuation though...'

'Pair of wankers.' Poke.

'Message deleted. Message three:' Bleeeeeep.

'Hello, Logan? It's Hamish.' The voice was a gravelly, breathless mix of Aberdonian and public school. Rattling at the edges where the cancer was eating him. *'I've been thinking about mortality. Yours. Mine. Reuben's. Everyone ... Give me a call back and we can talk about it.'*

The chip fat congealed at the back of Logan's throat. Crept forward and lined his mouth. Made his teeth itch. Wee Hamish Mowat. Not exactly the kind of message anyone wanted lying about on their answering machine where Professional Standards could find it.

And tell me, Acting DI McRae, would you care to explain why Aberdeen's biggest crime lord is phoning you for a chat, like an old mate?

No Logan sodding wouldn't. Poke.

'Message deleted. You have no new messages.'

Mortality.

With any luck, Wee Hamish had decided to save everyone the bother, and shot Reuben in the face.

Yeah, well. Probably not.

But a boy could dream, couldn't he?

— dearly beloved —

7

'… OK, let me know what you come up with. And for God's sake, someone give Guthrie a poke!'

The CID office had a full contingent of grey faces and wrinkly eyes. The four office chairs were lined up along two sides, turned towards the whiteboard for the morning briefing. Their occupants nursed tins of Irn-Bru and greasy bacon butties. Well, all except for PC Guthrie – slumped so far back in his seat that any further and he'd be on the floor. Gob open, head hanging to the side.

DS Baird leaned over and gave him a poke. 'You're snoring!'

Blinking, Guthrie surfaced, mouth working like a drowning fish. 'Mwake…'

Logan folded his arms and leaned back against the filing cabinet. 'Are we boring you, Constable?'

Wheezy Doug rolled his eyes. 'He wasn't even in the pub last night! No excuse.'

'Yeah.' DC Stone took another bite of buttie, talking with his mouth full. 'Should change your nickname from "Sunshine" to "Lightweight".' A little tuft of hair clung to the tip of Stoney's forehead, combed forward, backward, and sideways trying to hide a bald patch the size of a dinner plate. To be honest, Stoney's head was more bald patch than hair. As if trying to draw attention away from it, a huge moustache lurked beneath his nose like a hairy troll under a bridge. 'That right, Lightweight?'

Guthrie ran a hand over his face, scrubbing it out of shape. 'Just knackered from shagging your mum all night.'

That got him a collective, 'Oooh!'

Logan thumped a hand against the filing cabinet, setting it booming. 'All right, that's enough.' He pointed at the yawning constable. 'Where are we with Mrs Skinner?'

A shudder. Then Guthrie yawned. Pulled himself up in his seat. 'Still nothing from the lookout request. And she's not been back to the house since yesterday morning.'

'So where is she?'

Shrug. 'Neither set of grandparents had any idea. But, it's Sunday, right? Maybe she's gone to church? Or she stayed over at a friend's house? Slumber party for the kids?'

Logan frowned out of the window. Early morning sunlight painted the side of Marischal College, making the cleaned granite glow. They'd done their best – waited for her, put out a lookout request, contacted the next of kin. Sort of. What else were they supposed to do? If Mrs Skinner didn't want to be found, she didn't want to be found.

Maybe she knew her husband was working up to jumping off a dirty big building and decided to get out of town before he hit?

'Better get onto the Mire, Tayside, Highland, Fife, and Forth Valley – tell them to keep an eye out for her and the kids. Him diving off the casino roof's going to make the news sooner or later, and…' Logan closed his mouth.

Guthrie was shaking his head.

'What?'

The constable stood and crossed to one of the ancient

computers. 'I wasn't really shagging Stoney's mum all last night, I was checking the internet.' He thumped away at the keyboard. 'Three people loaded the footage up onto YouTube by midnight. I reported them, but it's already out there. See?' The screen filled with shaky cameraphone footage, looking up from Exchequer Row. The casino was five storeys of darkened windows, separated by strips of grey cladding. A figure stood on the roof – too far away to make out any detail on his face – arms by his sides, head down.

Muffled voices crackled from the speakers, *'Oh my God…'*, *'Look at him…'*, *'Is he going to jump?'*, *'Where? What are we looking at?'*, *'Oh my God…'*, *'Is that a knife?'*, *'Someone call the police!'*, *'Oh my God…'*

The scene swirled left, capturing the crowd. Most of them had their phones out, cameras pointing up at John Skinner as he wobbled on the edge.

Bloody vultures. Whatever happened to good Samaritans? *'There's someone else up there!'*, *'Oh my God…'*

A seasick lurch and the screen filled with the casino again as Logan inched his way out onto the ledge.

In real life, Logan pointed at the video. 'I want this taken down.'

'Oh my God…' A collective gasp as the green plastic bag from Markies kamikazed down to the cobbles, a bomb of crisps and sandwiches that exploded on impact. *'Someone has to call the police!'*, *'Oh my God…'*, *'This is so cool, it—'*

Logan jabbed at the mouse and the image froze. 'Get it deleted off the internet.'

Guthrie screwed up one side of his face. 'It's kinda gone viral, Guv. Copies popping up all over the place.'

'Then get out there and find me John Skinner's wife. *Now!*'

'I see.' Superintendent Young folded his hands behind his head and leaned back in the visitor's chair. He'd forgone his usual Police-Scotland-ninja-outfit for a pair of blue jeans and chunky trainers. A red T-shirt with 'SKELETON BOB IS MY COPILOT' on it under a grey hoodie. As if he was fourteen instead of forty. Forty something. Probably nearer fifty. 'And is Justin Robson going to pursue this?'

Logan shuffled a mess of paperwork into a stack and popped it in the out-tray. 'You didn't have to come in on your day off, Guv. I'm sure we can cope till Monday.'

'It's this, or clearing out the garage.' A shrug. 'Call me dedicated. So: Robson?'

'Well, it's civil, rather than criminal, so he'd have to take her to court. But he's got her bang to rights for defamation. Posters up all over the area saying he's a drug dealer? No way she'll wriggle out of it.'

'Hmm...' Young stuck his legs out and crossed his ankles, head back, looking up at the stained ceiling. 'On the one hand, if he *does* sue her it'll serve her right. Maybe make her rethink her obsession. On the other hand, it could tip her off the deep end.'

'Either way she's going to end up a bigger pain in our backsides.'

'True.' A shrug. 'Anything else you need my help with? This suicide victim's missing wife thing?'

Logan bared his teeth. 'Thanks, Guv, but I think you've helped enough.'

'Ah well, if you're sure.' Young stood. Stretched. Slumped. 'Suppose I'd better go clear out the garage. No rest for the saintly.' He paused, with one hand on the door. 'I hear you had a run in with Gordy Taylor yesterday?'

'Wants to drop the charges in exchange for two litres of whisky.'

'And so we support those brave souls who fight in our name...' A sigh. 'Right. Well, drop me a text or something.' Another pause. 'You're sure there's nothing else?'

Logan did his best to smile. 'Not unless you want to buy a one-bedroom flat?'

Logan licked his top lip. Stared down at his mobile phone. Couldn't put it off any longer. Well, he could, but it probably wasn't a great idea. He dug his thumbs into the back panel and slid the cover off. Prised out the battery and replaced the SIM card with a cheapy pay-as-you-go from the supermarket checkout loaded up with a whole fiver's worth of calls. Clicked everything back into place.

'Guv?'

When he looked up, Wheezy Doug was standing in the doorway, clutching a manila folder to his chest.

'Is it quick?'

A nod. Then a cough. Then a gargly clearing of the throat. 'Got the lookout request extended across all of Police Scotland. And the Media Office want clearance on a press release and poster.' He dug into the folder and came out with two sheets of paper. 'You want to OK them?'

Logan gave them a quick once-over, then handed both back. 'If they can figure out how to spell "Saturday" properly, tell them to run it.'

'Guv.' He put the sheets away. 'You hear they turfed Gordy Taylor out of hospital last night? Shouting and swearing and making an arse of himself.'

What a shock. 'Nothing broken when he got himself run over, then?'

'Nah. Lurched out the door and found himself some more booze. Uniform got a dozen complaints from Harlaw Road about him staggering about, knocking over bins and doing pretty much the same thing he'd been doing up at the hospital.' Wheezy sooked on his teeth for a bit. Then shook his head. 'I knew his dad. Decent enough bloke. Bit racist, with a drink in him, but other than that...'

'OK. Let me know if anyone spots Mrs Skinner.'

'Guv.'

Soon as Wheezy was gone, Logan grabbed his phone and headed out.

Sunlight sparkled back from the white granity mass of Marischal College, caught the wheeling seagulls and set them glowing against the blue sky. A taxi grumbled by, followed by a fat man on a bicycle wearing nowhere near enough Lycra to keep everything under control.

Logan nipped across the road, past the council headquarters and along Broad Street. Kept going onto the Gallowgate. Nice and casual. Up the hill, and right into the council car park in front of the squat DVLA building.

Nice and out of the way.

He pulled out his phone and dialled Wee Hamish's number. Listened to it ring.

And ring.

And ring.

That brittle, gravelly voice: *'Hello?'*

'Hamish. It's Logan McRae.'

'Ah, Logan. Yes. Good. How are you? How's that young lady of yours?'

'Still in a coma.' Strange how it didn't hurt to say that any more. Perhaps four years was long enough for it to scab over? 'What can I do for you, Hamish?'

'Is she getting all the help she needs, do you think?'

Logan wandered across the car park. 'The doctors and nurses are very good.'

'Oh I've got nothing but admiration for the NHS, believe me. They were very kind to my Juliette those last few months. But ... Maybe a private hospital would provide a more individual service? Where there's not so much pressure to meet performance targets.'

A path ran along the back of the car park, bordered by a wall. Logan leaned on it, looking down the hill to the dual carriageway and the big Morrisons. 'We got knocked back from Sunny Glen. No places.' A small laugh clawed its way out of his throat. 'Not that we can afford it. Anyway, it's too far away. I couldn't get all the way up to Banff to visit her every day. What's the point of that?'

'Hmm … I hear you're still trying to sell the flat. Any luck?'

'Hamish, you said you wanted to talk about Reuben.'

'Are you in financial difficulties, Logan, because if you are I'd be more than happy to lend—'

'No. I'm fine. I just … felt like selling the flat, that's all.'

'I thought you loved it there. Nice central location. And it's very convenient for work.'

'It's got memories I don't need.' Down below, an ambulance skirled its way along the dual carriageway, all lights blazing. 'Time for a change.'

'I understand.' There was a small pause, filled with a hissing noise, as if Wee Hamish was taking a hit from an aqualung. *'Would you like me to put in a word for you? There are a couple of neurology specialists I know who could help you find a place. Somewhere Samantha can get the individual attention she deserves. Let me see what I can do.'*

Logan tightened his grip on the phone. Puffed out a breath. 'What about you? How are you feeling?'

'I've been thinking about us *a lot recently. You, me, and Reuben. When I'm gone, he'll come after you. You're too big a threat for him to ignore.'*

'I'm not a threat! I keep telling—'

'It doesn't matter if you turn down the mantle or not, Logan. To Reuben you'll always be a threat.' Another hisssssssss. *'Would you like me to kill him for you?'*

All the moisture evaporated from Logan's mouth. 'What?'

'It would pain me, of course – he's been my right-hand man for a long, long time – but sometimes you have to sacrifice a rook to keep the game going.'

'Now, hold on—'

'Oh, it won't be until I'm gone. The least I can do is let him come to the funeral. But after that. Before he's had time to move against you…'

Logan turned away from the road. Squinted up at the DVLA's windows. No one looked back at him. Thank God. 'Hamish, I'm a police officer: I can't be part of a plot to *murder* someone! Not even Reuben.'

'Are you sure? He's more dangerous than you think.' This time, the hiss-filled pause stretched out into silence. Then: *'Well, perhaps that would be best. After all, if you're taking over the company, the staff will respect you more if you get rid of him yourself.'*

'That's not what I meant! It—'

'Don't leave it too long, Logan. When I die, the clock starts ticking.'

'You OK, Guv?' Guthrie lowered his pale eyebrows, making little wrinkles between them.

Logan sank into one of the CID office chairs. 'I nearly fell off a roof yesterday, my suit smells of drunk tramp, I'm dealing with a tree festooned with dog turds, I can't sell my flat, and I had an early-morning run-in with Professional Standards. I've had better days.'

A smile. 'Then I've got something that'll cheer you up.'

'Is it midget porn again? Because I've told you about that already.'

'Nope.' He held up his notebook. 'One dark-green Honda Jazz, parked on Newburgh Road, Bridge of Don. It's Emma Skinner's.'

Logan stood. 'Well, what are you sitting there for? Get a pool car!'

Newburgh Road was a twisting warren of identikit houses, buried away amongst all the other identikit housing developments on this side of the river. Some residents had added porches, or garages, but the same bland boxy stereotype shone through regardless.

Guthrie pointed through the windscreen at the blocky back end of a dark-green hatchback. 'Patrol car was out cruising for a pervert – been stealing knickers off washing lines – when the Honda pinged up on the ANPR.'

They parked behind it.

Logan climbed out into the sun and did a slow three-sixty. Nothing out of the ordinary. Just more beige architecture, the harling greyed by weather. 'Any idea which house?'

Guthrie locked up. 'Thought we'd door-to-door it. Can't be that far, can it?'

'Pffff...' Logan leaned back against a low garden wall and wiped a hand across his forehead. It came away damp. 'You *sure* that's her car?'

Guthrie took out his notebook and checked again. 'Number plate matches.'

'Then where the sodding hell is she?'

'Well, maybe—'

'Forty minutes! Wandering round like a pair of idiots, knocking on doors.' The scent of charring meat oozed out from a garden somewhere near, making his stomach growl. 'Starving now.'

Guthrie gave a big theatrical shrug. 'I don't get it. It's not like it'd be hard to find a parking space here, is it? You'd dump your car right outside the person you're visiting, right?'

'Unless you weren't supposed to be here. Didn't want people to see your car...' Logan pushed off the wall. 'We keep looking.'

'OK, thanks anyway.'

As soon as the auld mannie in the faded 'Britain's Next Big Star' T-shirt had closed the door, Logan stepped into the shade of a box hedge.

He ran a hand across the nape of his neck and wiped it dry on his trousers. Checked his watch. That was an hour they'd been at it now. Slogging their way along the road in the baking sun. Knocking on doors. Asking questions. Showing people the photo of Emma Skinner that Guthrie had found on Facebook. A selfie of Emma and her two kids, grinning away like lunatics, the background blocked out by the three of them. She had her blonde hair pulled back from her face, a half-inch of brown roots showing. A silver ring in her left nostril. An easy smile. Two small children with chocolate smudges covering half of their faces.

Logan loosened his tie.

A whole hour of shoving the photo under people's noses.

And still nothing.

Maybe she hadn't been visiting someone here after all? Maybe this was simply a convenient place to dump the car? Somewhere to keep it hidden.

Why? Why would she want to hide?

'Guv?' One house over, Guthrie was backing away from the door – a hand scrabbling at the Airwave clipped to his stabproof vest. 'Guv!'

Logan hopped the low garden wall and hurried across a manicured lawn ringed with nasturtiums. 'Someone spotted her?'

Guthrie stopped in the middle of the path and pointed at the house. 'In there...'

OK.

He walked over to the front window. It was too bright outside, and too dark inside to see anything other than the reflected street scene. Logan cupped his hands either side of his eyes and pressed his forehead against the glass.

A high-heeled shoe lay in front of a glass-topped coffee table. On its side. The foot it belonged to poked out from behind the couch. Skin pale, a thick line of purple running horizontal with the ground where the blood had settled. More blood on the oatmeal-coloured carpet. Little dots and splashes. Dozens of them. More streaking up the walls, making scarlet spatters across a print of the New York skyline.

Definitely dead.

8

'Got you ham-cheese-and-mustard, and a tin of Lilt.' Guthrie held out a Tesco carrier bag.

Sitting back against the pool car, Logan dipped into the bag. 'Crisps?'

'Cheese-and-onion.'

Better than nothing. 'Thanks.'

A cordon of blue-and-white 'POLICE' tape cut across Newburgh Road, keeping the scene secure – enclosing the house, a patrol car, and the Scenes Examination Branch's dirty transit van. At least someone'd had the brains to scrub a hand through the filthier bits of finger graffiti.

Guthrie got stuck into an egg-and-cress, making mayonnaise smears either side of his mouth. 'Starving…'

Logan clicked the ring-pull off his fizzy juice, and chased down a mouthful of sandwich. Then wiggled the can towards the house. 'Looks like we're on.'

A pair of figures stepped out of the front door, both done up in full SOC Smurf outfits – blue booties, white Tyvek suit, blue nitrile gloves, facemasks, and eye goggles. Smurf One was tall and lanky, Smurf Two shorter with an itchy bum. Smurf Two dug and scratched away at its backside as the pair of them made their way across to the pool car.

Logan took another bite, talking with his mouth full. 'Well?'

DI Steel peeled her suit's hood back, then pulled off the mask and let it dangle beneath her chin. 'Sodding roasting...' Her face was a florid shade of red, the skin streaked with glistening lines of sweat. She stuck out her gloved hands, groping for Logan's Lilt. 'Give.' Then glugged away at it as Smurf One unfurled his suit and tied the arms around his waist.

Detective Sergeant Simon Rennie puffed out his cheeks and sagged. Wafted a hand in front of his flushed shiny face. Being inside the hood had done something terrible to his hair, leaving the blond mop sticking out at all angles, like a confused hedgehog. 'Gah...'

Logan tried again. 'Is it her?'

Steel gulped. Puffed out a long breath. Then burped. 'God, that's better.'

Rennie held out the picture Guthrie found on Facebook. 'It's her. Multiple stab wounds to the chest and abdomen – and I mean *multiple*. Has to be at least forty.' He rubbed a forearm across his face, blotting away the sweat. 'Don't have another tin of juice, do you?'

Steel handed him whatever was left of Logan's. 'There's a naked bloke in the bedroom too. Throat cut from ear to ear. Place looks like something out of a B-movie slasher; it's dripping from the ceiling and everything.'

A sigh escaped from Logan's chest. 'Let me guess – she's naked too.'

'Nope: kinky bra with matching thong.'

Which explained why Emma Skinner had parked so far away. Didn't want anyone to see her visiting her lover.

Mr Suicide's voice trembled, not much more than a broken whisper. 'How could she do *that?'* It explained that as well.

63

The lover had to die, but the wife had to be *punished*.

'We've had the murder weapon since yesterday.' Logan pointed towards the house. 'Anyone want to bet you'll find John Skinner's fingerprints all over the place? He follows her here, he catches her in the act, slits the lover's throat, then goes berserk with the knife. Can't live with what he's done, so he chucks himself off the casino roof, still clutching the knife.'

'Aye, well done Jonathan Creek.' Steel snatched the Lilt back from Rennie and tipped her head back. Frowned. Shook the can a couple of times. 'You greedy little sod!'

'You didn't say I couldn't finish it.'

'You don't glug back the last of someone else's *drink*. Everyone knows that.' She unzipped her SOC suit. 'Idiot.' Then snapped off her gloves. 'Got sweat trickling right down the crack of my—'

'What about the kids?' Logan nodded towards the picture in Rennie's hand. Those two chocolatey faces. 'Mrs Skinner takes them to their school clubs, Saturday morning, drives over here to see her lover. Her *husband* follows her and kills the pair of them, then drives back into town and jumps off the casino roof. Where are the kids?'

Steel closed her eyes. 'Crap.' She massaged her forehead for a moment. Then straightened up. 'Right, finding the kids is now *everyone's* number one priority. I want lookout requests, I want posters, I want media appeals...' She frowned. 'What?'

Logan popped his half-eaten sandwich back in the packet. 'Already done it. Media office are holding off till you've delivered the death message, but other than that they're ready to go.'

'Oh.' A sniff. 'In that case: Laz, you get started on the paperwork, and I'll—'

'Oh no you don't.' Logan held up a hand. 'You took the

case over, remember? Turned up here all lights blazing and said it was too *complicated* for us thickies in CID – this was a job for the Major Investigation Team. Remember that?'

She shuffled her feet. Looked off into the distance. 'Yeah, well, I may have been a bit overenthusiastic with—'

'Do your own sodding paperwork.'

'You're no' *still* sulking, are you?' Steel leaned against Logan's office doorway, arms folded, a 'WORLD'S GREATEST LESBIAN' mug dangling from the fingers of one hand.

He turned back to the duty roster, typing in the team's work plan for the next shift. 'Away and boil your head.'

'You're going to have to learn to share, Laz.'

'Share?' He thumped away at the keyboard, making it suffer. 'You turn up, you tell us we're crap, then you take the case away – even though we've already *solved* it – and grab all the sodding credit.'

A sniff. 'Yeah, but I had to do all the paperwork.'

He stared at her. 'Did you really? Or did you get Rennie to do it?'

A little blush coloured her cheeks. 'I supervised.'

Back to the roster. 'Feel free to sod off any time you like.'

She did. But she was back three minutes later with a steaming mug in each hand, a packet of biscuits tucked under her arm, and a Jaffa Cake poking out of her mouth. 'Mmmnnphh, gnnnph, mmmmnph?'

One of the mugs got placed on the desk in front of him. Then the biscuits.

He scowled at them. 'What's this?'

'Peace offering.' She sank into one of the visitors' chairs. 'Between friends.'

'What are you after?'

'Me? Nothing.' A shrug and a smile. 'Can't two old friends share a cuppa and a digestive biscuit or two?'

He picked up the mug and sniffed. It smelled like tea, but it looked like coffee. 'What happened to the Jaffa Cakes?'

'Yeah, they're all gone.' She plonked her feet up on his desk. 'So, double murder solved in an hour and a half. Not bad going.'

'Are you seriously sitting there gloating about solving a case that *I* solved for you?'

'Moan, bitch, whinge.' She crunched a bite out of her digestive, getting crumbs all down the front of her shirt. 'You're such a princess.'

'I am *not* a sodding princess.'

'Whatever you say, Your Majesty.' More crumbs. Steel stared out of the window, then her shoulders dropped a little. 'Still no sign of the kids.'

'Early days yet.'

'Got a press conference at half six, going out live on the news. No' exactly looking forward to that. Come Monday morning, going to be like a siege out there.' She took a slurp of tea. Finished her biscuit. Offered him the packet. 'So … You busy Tuesday night?'

'Here we go.'

'Only it's Susan and me's anniversary, and if you're no' too busy sitting at home like a sad sack, you could look after Jasmine for the night. Be nice for you to spend a bit more time with your daughter.'

Logan saved the file, then closed down the computer. 'How come you only think I need to spend more time with Jasmine when you need a free babysitter?'

'Think of it – I'm going to wheech Susan off to a swanky hotel, get room service to deliver champagne and strawberries, put a bit of porn on the telly, then shag her brains out.' Steel flicked biscuit crumbs out of her own cleavage. 'Very romantic.'

'I'm busy Tuesday.'

'No you're no'.'

'Yes I am.'

'Doing what?'

'I've got … a viewing. Someone's coming round to look at the flat.'

'No they're no'. You're going to be sitting at home, watching *The Little Mermaid*, in your pants, with your cat. Nipping off for a touch of onanism when singing along to "Part of Your World" gets you a bit horny.'

A knock on the door and Wheezy Doug stuck his head in.

Oh thank God.

'Guv? It's Mrs Black – just called nine-nine-nine.'

Maybe not. Logan folded forwards until his forehead rested on the keyboard. 'It's *home* time.'

'Yeah, but she says her neighbour's trying to kill her with a cleaver.'

The siren shredded the early evening air as their pool car slewed around onto Pitmedden Court.

Steel latched onto the grab handle above the passenger door as the front wheels hit a speed bump, wheeching them into the air like something off the *Streets of San Francisco*. 'Yeeeeeeee-ha!'

The car slammed down onto the tarmac again, with a grinding groan.

Sitting in the back, Logan reached out and slapped Wheezy Doug over the back of the head. 'What did I tell you?'

'Sorry, Guv, urgent threat to life and that.' He kept his foot down.

Mrs Black's thick leylandii hedge appeared in the middle distance, rushing up to meet them as Wheezy screeched the car to a halt, nose in to the kerb. He grabbed a high-viz waistcoat and jumped out, struggling into the thing as he ran across the pavement.

Logan scrambled after him, charging up the path to Mrs Black's house as Wheezy slid the front down on his body-worn video, setting it recording.

BANG – Justin Robson battered his bare foot into his neighbour's front door. 'YOU BITCH! YOU BLOODY VINDICTIVE BLOODY BITCH!' His Bagpuss sweat pants billowed as he drew back for another kick, camouflage T-shirt stained beneath the armpits. The same dirty big kitchen knife as last time, clutched in one hand. 'COME OUT HERE!'

Logan stopped, a good six foot shy of the huge blade. 'Mr Robson? I need you to calm down for me.'

BANG. Another kick. 'I'LL BLOODY KILL YOU!'

Wheezy dragged out a canister of CS gas. Held the other hand out in front of him, palm out. 'Mr Robson, it's the police. Drop the knife. *Now*.'

Robson turned. Chest heaving. Mouth a wet wobbly line. Glasses steamed up. 'Did you see what that BITCH did to my car? Did you?' Back to the house. 'YOU RANCID, VINDICTIVE, BLOODY BITCH!'

Wheezy raised the canister. 'Ever been gassed, Mr Robson? It's not nice. And you're going to find out what it feels like if you don't *drop the bloody knife*!'

He looked down at the cleaver, as if seeing it for the first time. Then let go. Backed up a pace, hands up as it clattered on the paving slabs. Cleared his throat. 'OK, OK, there's no need for that. This is all a big misunder— ulk!'

Wheezy grabbed him by the camouflage and spun him into the closed front door. Shoved his head against the UPVC. Stuffed the canister of CS gas back where it came from as he whipped out the cuffs. Snapped them on Robson's wrists. Dragged him away down the path.

'Get off me!' Robson shook his head left and right, like a dog with a rat. 'It's *her* you should be arresting, not me. Look what she did to my car!'

Logan pulled a blue nitrile glove from his pocket and snapped it on. Bent and picked up the fallen knife. Carried it out to the kerb.

'Look at my car...'

Justin Robson's white BMW wasn't so white any more. What looked like gloss paint Jackson Pollocked across the roof, windscreen, and bonnet in bright splatters of pink and yellow and blue, running in rainbow tears down the wings. The words 'Drug Dealer!!!' were scratched into the bodywork, over and over again, gouged deep enough to crease the raw metal underneath.

'Look at it...'

The sound of someone sooking on a tube appeared at Logan's shoulder, followed by a puff of vapour. Steel did a slow circuit of the vandalized BMW. 'No' the colour I would've chosen, but it makes a statement.'

Logan took the knife around to the pool car's boot, unzipped the holdall in there and pulled out a knife tube. He slipped the cleaver inside the clear plastic tube and sealed it. Marched back to where Wheezy held the sagging man. 'Right, Justin Robson, I'm arresting you for breach of the peace, possession of a deadly weapon, attempted breaking and entering, attempted—'

'We get it.' Steel worked her e-cigarette from one side of her mouth to the other. Nodded at Robson. 'You: Bagpuss. Tweedle Dum and Tweedle Dee here tell me you're on a feud with her next door.'

'She's *insane*.'

'Don't care.' A yellowed finger pointed in Logan's direction. 'Tweedle Dee – get this wifie...?'

He stared back at her. 'Marion Black.'

'Don't care. You get Wifie Black out here and we'll see if Saint Roberta of Steel can't pour some baby oil on these troubled waters. Amen, and all that.'

He didn't even try to suppress the groan. 'Seriously?'

'Finger out, Laz, got bigger fish to fry than this pair of idiots.' She checked her watch. 'Got to be on telly in an hour. Chop, chop.'

Fine. Wasn't as if they didn't have to take Mrs Black's statement anyway.

He turned and marched back up the path. Gave the front door the policeman's knock – three, loud and hard. 'Mrs Black?'

A thin voice came from the other side of the door. 'Who is it?'

'It's the police.' As if the pool car sitting out front with its blue lights flashing wasn't enough of a clue. 'I need you to open up.'

'Not if he's still out there. Is he still out there?'

'Mr Robson is in custody at the moment, so if…'

The door sprang open. Mrs Black stood on the threshold in her dressing gown and jammies, even though it couldn't have been much more than twenty past five. She had a fire iron in both hands, clutched against her chest. 'He's a menace. I *told* you he was dangerous!' She grinned up at Logan. The whites were visible all the way around her bulging eyes. 'I told you, but you wouldn't listen. Said there wasn't any proof.' The words rolled out on a cloud of second-hand alcohol. She shifted from one slippered foot to the other. 'Is this proof enough for you? *Is* it?'

'I need you to come talk to the Detective Chief Inspector.'

At that, Mrs Black pulled herself up straight, shoulders back. 'About time I got to speak to *someone* in authority.' She brushed past him, shuffling up the path.

Then froze as she reached the pavement and spotted DCI Steel. 'Where is he then? This Detective Chief Inspector?'

Steel sniffed. Howched. And spat into the gutter. 'Bit sexist, isn't it?'

Yeah, this was definitely going to end well.

Robson glowered out from behind his squint glasses. 'You vicious, scheming—'

Wheezy must have done something painful to him, because his eyes screwed shut and whatever word came next got replaced by a hiss.

A nod. Then Mrs Black's grin darkened. 'See? He's *dangerous*. He's a drug dealer and he tried to kill me and now you've got to lock him up for the rest of his perverted unnatural life, and—'

'She planned this! Can't you see she planned it? It's all a set-up—'

'—prison and that's where you belong you—'

'—vandalized my car! She *knew* I loved—'

A harsh, shrill whistle ripped the air and everyone went quiet.

A handful of neighbours had drifted into their front gardens. Suddenly consumed by an overpowering need to trim their hedges, or prune a rose bush. All of them frozen by the whistle.

Steel took two fingers from her mouth and wiped them on her rumpled suit jacket. 'Better.' She turned a shark smile on Mrs Black. 'Did you, or did you no', trash this man's car?'

The nose came up. 'I did nothing of the sort.'

'So, when I get my two colleagues here to search your property, they're no' going to find any paint tins? White spirit? Stained clothes or shoes?'

Mrs Black's mouth pursed at that last one. She looked out across the gardens. 'He tried to kill me.'

'Thought so: they never get rid of the shoes.' Steel turned the smile on Robson. 'And did you, Justin Robson, attempt to stab Mrs Black to death?'

Pink rushed up his cheeks. He stared down at his bare feet. 'She trashed my car, I was … only trying to … Was carving the Sunday roast when I saw what she did.' A shrug. 'Forgot I was holding the knife...'

'And does anyone here present have any just reason why I shouldn't throw the book at you pair of silly sods and let the courts decide?' Steel made a gun out of her fingers and shot Mrs Black in the face. 'Criminal damage.' Then did the same to Robson. 'Aggravated assault. Minimum eight months apiece. That what you want?'

Neither of them said anything.

'Because if I hear so much as a *whisper* that you've been sodding about like this again, I'm going to bury the Great Leather Shoe of God in both your arses.'

Silence.

She shot Robson again. 'Do you understand?'

He shifted his feet. Turned his head to the side. 'I do.'

Mrs Black got another finger bullet. 'You?'

A pause. Then she lowered her eyes and nodded. 'Yes. Fine. No more fighting.'

Steel raised her arms, as if delivering a benediction. 'Then by the powers vested in me by the High Heid Yins of Police Scotland, I hereby declare this feud *over*.'

— they never get rid of the shoes —

9

Stoney eased into the room, a folder balanced on the palm of one hand acting as a tray for a mound of tinfoil-wrapped packages. 'Three bacon, one sausage, and one booby-trapped. Get them while they're hot.'

The rest of the team swarmed him, snatching up their butties, then retreating to their seats to unwrap them. The air filled with the meaty smoky scents.

Early morning light oozed through the dirty office window, turning it nearly opaque, hiding the pre-rush-hour calm of a slowly waking Aberdeen.

Logan checked his watch: five past seven. Time to get going. He ripped a bite of sausage buttie and pointed at the whiteboard. 'Guthrie?'

At least he didn't look *quite* so much like an extra from *Night of the Living Dead* this morning.

'Mrs Skinner's boyfriend was a Brian Williams. Twenty-two. Engineer with TransWell Subsea Systems in Portlethen. Steel's MIT took over the investigation, but I still had to deliver the sodding death message to his fiancée. She wasn't too chuffed.'

Wheezy Doug picked at his teeth. 'There's a shock.'

'Here's a bigger one – the MIT are taking all the credit.'

DS Baird frowned at the whiteboard for a moment, then wiped a smear of tomato sauce from her cheek. 'Got a good write-up in the paper, though.' She picked a copy of the *Aberdeen Examiner* from her desk and held it up.

The front page had a more formal photograph than the one Logan and Guthrie had been showing around yesterday. A posed family portrait with a marbly background. Everyone in their Sunday best, hair combed, teeth shiny. 'FAMILY FEARS FOR MISSING CHILDREN'.

Baird cleared her throat and turned the paper back to face herself. '"It wasn't as if the Skinner family didn't have enough tragedy to deal with. On Saturday, John Skinner – thirty-five – jumped to his death, and on Sunday, his wife of eight years, Emma Skinner – twenty-seven – was found stabbed to death in a family home in the Bridge of Don. But what hurts most, say John and Emma's parents, is that Heidi – seven – and Toby – six – are missing…"' Baird wrinkled her top lip. 'Why are the papers obsessed with how old people are? What's the point?'

Wheezy stuffed down another bite of buttie, talking with his mouth full. 'They say anything about us?'

She skimmed the front page, lips moving silently as she went. 'Nope. "Detective Chief Inspector Roberta Steel…" See they haven't got *her* age. "…told a press conference yesterday that Police Scotland was very concerned for the children's safety. 'We will leave no stone unturned in our quest to find Heidi and Toby…'" Blah, blah, blah. Nothing about you, or the Guvnor.'

'Typical.'

A little yellow trail of yolk was making its way down Guthrie's chin. 'Guv, are you still interested in Gordy Taylor?'

'Wasn't interested in him in the first place.'

'Only the girl who gave him a kicking's up before the Sheriff at twenty past nine.'

76

'Pleading guilty?'

'Blaming it on PMS and starting university.'

Baird shuddered. '*Hate* women who do that. "Oh, I can't act rationally, because I'm a weak and feeble woman at the mercy of my hormonal uterus." Puts the whole cause back a hundred years.'

Logan held up his hand. 'Right, soon as everyone's finished their buttie, I want—' His phone blared out the anonymous ringtone that signalled an unknown caller. 'Give us a minute.' He pulled it out and hit the button. 'DI McRae.'

Screaming battered out of the earpiece and he flinched back.

Then tried again. 'Hello? Who is this?'

The screaming broke into jagged words, roughened by sobs. *'He's killed them all!'*

'There! Look what he did. LOOK AT THEM!' Mrs Black's trembling finger came up and pointed at the back fence.

The back garden stank of ammonia. It turned every breath into a struggle, caught the back of the throat, made the air taste of sour vinegar and dirt. Logan blinked tears from his stinging eyes.

Cages ran down one side of the long garden, backing onto the massive leylandii hedge between this side and Justin Robson's house on the other. Wooden frames with metal mesh inserts, full of perches and floored with sawdust and droppings. Every single door hung open.

But they weren't what Mrs Black was pointing at.

About twenty little bodies were frozen against the back fence – wings out. Most were blue with white faces, but some were green-and-yellow instead. And each one had a large nail hammered through its breast, pinning it to the wood. As if a butterfly collector had decided his hobby just wasn't creepy enough and it was time to upgrade to something bigger.

Blood made spattered patterns on the fence behind and beneath them.

Mrs Black sobbed, tears coating her cheeks, gulping down air only to cry it out again. 'My *babies*…'

'OK.' A nod. 'Is Mr Black—'

'Don't you … don't you *dare* mention … mention that *bastard's* name.' She ground the heel of her hand into her eye sockets. 'He walked out on me. On ME! Packed his bags like *I* was the one being unreasonable.' She threw her arms out. 'LOOK AT IT! LOOK WHAT HAPPENED!' The arms drooped by her sides. 'My babies…'

Logan puffed out a breath. Then patted Wheezy Doug on the shoulder. 'Constable Andrews, maybe you should get Mrs Black inside and make a cup of tea, or something. I'm going next door.'

Justin Robson folded his arms and leaned back against the kitchen counter. 'Nope. Nothing to do with me.' His face was pale with greeny-purple bags under the eyes, his breath stale and bitter. Hair slicked back and wet. Dark-blue dressing gown.

Behind him, the garden was in darkness, the early morning sunshine murdered by Mrs Black's spite hedge. A curl of smoke twisted up into the gloom.

Logan pulled out his notebook. 'Come off it: she trashes your car, and you decide to turn the other cheek? *Really*?'

'Wasn't even here: out all night at a friend's house. You can check if you like.'

'Oh we will.' The pen hovered over the pad. 'Name?'

'Can do you better than that. Hold on, I'll call him.' Robson picked the phone out of its cradle and fiddled with the buttons. The sound of ringing blared out of the speaker.

Then, *click*. *'Hello?'*

'Bobby? It's Justin. Sorry to call so early, but can you tell this guy where I was last night?' He held out the phone.

'What? Yeah, Justin came round about six-ish? We watched a couple of films. Had a bit too much wine and a moan about girls till about three in the morning. Justin was so blootered he could barely stand.'

'Cheeky sod. No I wasn't.'

'Were. So I put him in the spare room. Set the alarm. And went to bed.'

Logan wrote it all down. At least that explained the pallor and the smell. 'And he didn't leave the house?'

'No way Justin could've got out without deactivating the alarm and he doesn't know the code. Didn't go home till about half an hour ago? Forty-five minutes? Something like that? Told him he should cop a sicky and crash here all morning, but blah-blah work etc.'

A nice tight alibi. Very convenient. 'OK, I'm going to need your full name and address.'

Wheezy Doug snapped off his blue nitrile gloves and stuffed them into a carrier bag. 'What kind of dick does that to harmless wee birds?'

Logan nodded back towards the house with the decorated cherry tree. 'How is she?'

'Mangled. Says that after her husband stormed out, she hit the vodka. Staggered off to bed about eleven after checking the birds were all fine. Gets up at seven this morning and finds *that*.' Wheezy puffed out his cheeks. 'Poor wee things. I had to lever them off the fence with a claw-hammer. That's why some are a bit squashed.' He pulled out a pen and printed the evidence label for twenty parakeets, all sharing a big evidence pouch. Each one individually zip-locked into its own tiny plastic bag. 'What about laughing boy?'

'Says he had nothing to do with it. Got himself an alibi.'

'That's convenient.' Wheezy closed the pool car's boot.

'Exactly what I thought.' Logan led the way back to the house.

Robson had moved through to the lounge, a bowl of Rice Krispies in his lap. Breakfast News burbled away on the widescreen telly as he tied a tie around his pale neck. He'd swapped the dressing gown for trainers, jeans, and a pale-yellow shirt.

'... *double murder in Aberdeen yesterday have been identified as Emma Skinner and Brian Williams...*'

He straightened his tie, then dipped a spoon into his cereal. 'You forget something?'

'... *committed suicide on Saturday.*' The screen filled with amateur mobile-phone video of John Skinner preparing to jump.

Logan stepped between Robson and the TV as the anchor handed over to Carol for the weather. 'You do understand that we can take DNA from the parakeets, don't you? Whoever killed them will have left their DNA on their feathers. We'll get it from the nails too. *And* fingerprints.'

'Isn't science marvellous.'

'We can match contact traces of metal between the nail-heads and a specific hammer. We can match the nails with ones from the same batch.'

'OK.' He killed the TV, then put his breakfast on the coffee table. 'Tell you what, if you don't believe I was with Bobby all night, why don't you search the house again? Do the garden too. You can even try the shed.'

Little sod was either innocent, or arrogant enough to believe he could get away with it.

Wheezy Doug tucked his hands into his pockets and nodded at Robson's feet. The trainers were bright white, without so much as a scuff on them. 'They're nice. Look new.'

'Cool, aren't they? Fresh on today.'

'Where are the old ones?'

He smiled. 'Yeah, they were getting all stinky and dirty. Plus, someone *might* have been sick on them last night. So I got rid of them.'

What a surprise. Nothing quite so incriminating as a pair of blood-stained Nikes.

Logan took out his notebook. 'And where, *exactly*, are these sick-drenched shoes now? In the bin?'

'Ah...' Robson bared his top teeth in a rabbit grin. 'I burned them soon as I got home. Was doing some garden rubbish anyway.' He stood and walked through to the kitchen. Pointed out through the window to a stainless-steel bin, hidden away in the shadows at the bottom of the garden. The thing had holes in its sides and a chimney lid. Coils of smoke drifted away into the morning sky. 'Never had one before, but it's *really* efficient. Burns everything.'

Definitely arrogant. And probably right.

Robson frowned. 'You know, now I think about it, if I'd been nailing live parakeets to a fence, I'd be all covered with scratches and pecks, wouldn't I?' He held up his hands. Not a single mark on them. 'I mean, they're going to put up a fight, aren't they?'

Logan stepped in close. 'This stops and it stops here. No more. Understand?'

The smile didn't slip an inch. 'Nothing to do with me. You'd have to speak to the bitch next door.'

Yeah, there was no way this was over.

'We'll be watching you, Mr Robson.' Logan turned and marched from the room, down the hall and out the front door.

Wheezy Doug hurried after him. Unlocked the pool car and slipped in behind the wheel. 'He did it, didn't he?'

'Course he did. He doesn't have scratches on his hands, because he wore gloves. And then he burned them. So no

81

fingerprints on the nails or the birds. And odds on he'd wear a facemask too.'

'So no DNA, or good as.'

'Bet he even burned the hammer.' Logan stared back at the house.

Robson was standing in the living room, smiling through the window. He gave them a wave.

Logan didn't wave back. 'This is going to get worse before it gets better.'

Wheezy pulled away from the kerb. 'And last time we were here, I distinctly remember DCI Steel making a big thing of how no one ever gets rid of their shoes. The wee turd listened and learned.'

Logan took his Airwave handset from his jacket pocket. 'Should've arrested them both when we had probable cause.' Too late for that now though, it'd been no-crimed. He pressed the talk button. 'DI McRae to Control. I need a Wildlife Crime Officer, or whatever it is we're calling them these days.'

Twenty dead parakeets.

Yeah, this was definitely going to get a *lot* worse.

10

Baird dipped into the big evidence bag and came out with a wee, individually wrapped, dead parakeet. Wrinkled her nose. 'Poor thing.'

Logan's office was warmer than it had any right to be. He cracked open the window, letting in a waft of stale air tainted by cigarette smoke. 'Killed all twenty of them.'

She placed it back in the bag with the others. 'Twenty dead little bodies.'

'If you were Mrs Black, what would you do?'

'Me?' Baird scrunched her lips into a duck pout. 'If I was a total nutjob, what would I do? Cut his knackers off. No, not cut, I'd *hack* them off. With a rusty spoon.'

Logan sank into his seat. 'That's what worries me.' He pointed at the big bag. 'Get it off to the labs. I want anything they can get linking the birds to Justin Robson before this goes any further. At least if one of them's banged up they can't kill each other.'

'Guv.' She picked it up. 'What about the Skinner kids?'

'No idea.'

'Seems a shame, doesn't it? Wasn't their fault their mum was screwing around.'

'Never is.' Logan pulled his keyboard over. 'If the lab gives you stick about analysing a bunch of parakeets, tell them I'll be round to insert a size nine up their jacksy next time I've got a minute. It's—'

A knock on the door and there was Guthrie, face all pink and shiny, out of breath as if he'd been running. 'Guv … It's … It's…' He folded over and grabbed his knees for a bit. 'Argh … God…'

Baird patted him on the back. 'That's what you get for eating so much cheese, Sunshine.'

He shook her off and had another go. 'Guv, it's … Gordy Taylor…'

Logan groaned. 'What's he done now?'

'Dead…'

Baird dumped the evidence bag back on Logan's desk. 'I'll get a pool car.'

Baird tucked her hair into the SOC suit's hood, then pulled the zip up all the way to her chin. Grabbed a handful of material around the waist and hoiked it up, setting the white Tyvek rustling. 'You ready?'

Behind her, a double line of blue-and-white 'Police' tape cut off a chunk of Harlaw Road, tied between trees on opposite sides of the street, casting a snaking shadow. A crime scene dappled with light falling through the leaves.

The houses on the opposite side of the street didn't look all that fancy – detached granite bungalows with attic conversions and dormer windows – but they overlooked the green expanse of the playing fields, so probably cost an absolute fortune.

Logan snapped a second set of blue nitrile gloves on over the first. 'Might as well.'

They ducked under the outer cordon and rustled their way across the tarmac to the inner boundary of yellow-and-black

– 'CRIME SCENE – DO NOT CROSS' – where a spotty uniform with huge eyes demanded to see their ID then wrote their names in the log before letting them past.

Two large council bins were lined up against the kerb, and behind them someone in the full Smurf outfit was squatting beside the body. He had a bony wrist in one hand, turning it over, letting the attached filthy hand flop one way, then the other.

Logan sank down next to him, blinking at the stench of alcohol and baked sewage. 'Doc.'

The figure looked up and nodded – more or less anonymous behind the facemask and safety goggles. 'Well, it's official: this gentleman's definitely dead.'

He let go of the wrist and shuffled back, letting them get a proper look at the body.

Gordon Taylor lay curled up on his side; knees drawn up to his chest; one arm thrown back, the hand dangling against his spine; the other reaching out in front. Head twisted back, mouth open. Eyes glazed. Beard and hair matted with twigs and vomit.

A bluebottle landed on Gordon's cheek, and the Duty Doctor wafted it away. 'Well, there's no sign of serious trauma. He's not been stabbed, or bludgeoned to death. The only sign of blood is that…' The doctor pointed at the grubby bandage wrapped around Gordon's right hand. It was stained with dark-scarlet blobs.

'You want to guess at time of death?'

'Very roughly? Sometime between him getting chucked out of hospital, and the bin men finding him here this morning.' A shrug. 'Anyone who gives you anything more precise is a liar.'

'Any sign of foul play?'

'Doubt it: your friend here choked on his own vomit. If you want *my* opinion, you're looking at what happens when you spend your life downing litre bottles of supermarket vodka, whisky, and gin. Sooner or later it catches up with you.' He straightened up with a groan and rubbed at the small of his back. 'And with that, the brave Duty Doctor's work was done, and he could get back to treating hypochondriac morons who think they know better than him because they've looked leprosy up on the internet.'

The uniform with the spots held up the barrier tape and the undertaker's plain grey van eased back out onto Harlaw Road. The driver nodded to Logan and drove off.

Wheezy Doug was in conversation with a middle-aged man with a walking stick, two houses down. Stoney was at the far end of the street, nodding and taking notes as a mother of two waved her arms about, a pair of red-haired kids running screaming around her legs. DS Baird wandered up the road, hands in her pockets.

She stopped beside Logan and nodded at the departing van. 'That him off, then?'

'You get anything?'

'Far as we can tell, Gordon Taylor's been hanging around here for about a fortnight. I got Control to pull anything relating to Harlaw Road and three streets either side. There's been an increase in breaking and enterings: low-level stuff, shed padlocks forced, meths and white spirit nicked kind of thing. One stolen handbag – owner put it on the roof of her car while she unloaded the shopping, came back: no handbag. Loads of complaints of antisocial behaviour.' She pulled out her notebook and flipped it open at the marker. 'And I quote, "There's a smelly tramp staggering up and down the street at all hours, singing filthy rugby songs and rummaging through the bins."' Baird turned the page. 'Eight counts of public urination. No one ever caught him at it, but in the morning people's doorways would smell of piddle. That lot,' she pointed at a tidy house with an immaculate garden, where a little old lady was pruning a rosebush, 'called the police eight times in the last week.'

Well, the old dear wasn't so much pruning the bush as nipping *tiny* bits off the one branch, probably using it as an excuse to have a nosy. She wasn't the only one. At least half a dozen others were out, taking their time washing cars or raking the lawn. Pretending not to snoop.

A glazier's van sat outside the old lady's house. The driver and his mate were in the cab, stuffing down chocolate biscuits and pouring tea from a thermos. Staring as if this was the most interesting thing to happen all day. An episode of *Taggart*, playing out right there in front of them.

Logan turned his back on the gawkers. 'So what happened?'

Baird shrugged. 'Patrol car did a drift by a couple of times, but you know what it's like. Don't have time to attend every moaning numpty.'

True. But if they'd *actually* done something about it – if they'd turned up and arrested him – Gordon Taylor would probably still be alive today. Hard to drink yourself to death in a police cell.

Something heavy settled behind Logan's eyes, pulling his whole head down.

And if *he'd* arrested Gordon Taylor on Saturday for being drunk and incapable, or done him for biting two security guards and a nurse, or for punching that other nurse on the nose...

Pfff...

'You OK, Guv?'

A one-shouldered shrug. 'Missed opportunities.' He looked off down the road.

Didn't really matter in the end, did it? Lock Gordon Taylor up for a night, or a week, and he'd still hit the bottle as soon as he got out. All it would've done was delay the inevitable. Sooner or later, he'd be in the undertaker's van on the way to the mortuary.

Logan dragged in a deep breath, then let it out. Checked his watch. Might as well head back to the office and do something productive. 'Get Wheezy to deliver the death message. He knows Gordon Taylor's dad. Might be better if he finds out from a friend.'

There was only so much you could do.

Logan spat the last cold dregs of coffee back into his mug and shuddered. Time for a fresh cup.

He'd got as far as his office door when his mobile launched into its anonymous ringtone. Please let it be anyone other than Mrs Sodding Black again.

He hit the button. 'McRae.'

'Mr McRae? It's Marjory from Willkie and Oxford, Solicitors? How are you doing? That's great. I've had Mr and Mrs Moore on the phone again and they're prepared to go as far as fifteen thousand below the valuation.'

'Then Mr and Mrs Moore can go screw themselves.'

A fake laugh came down the phone as Logan let himself out into the corridor, making for the stairwell. *'Well, I had to let you know anyway. I'll get back to their solicitor. And I wanted to know if you're available this afternoon? We've had a call from a young man interested in viewing the property.'*

'I'm on duty.' Which part of serving police officer did she not understand?

'Right. Yes. Well, not to worry, I can show him around.'

Nice to know she'd be doing something for her one-percent-cut of the price.

He slid his phone back in its pocket and clumped up the stairs to the canteen. Froze in the doorway.

DCI Steel sat at the table in front of the vending machine, working her way through a Curly Wurly and a tin of Coke.

A large parcel lay on the floor at her feet, wrapped in brown paper and about a mile of packing tape. She hadn't seen him yet – too busy chewing. All he had to do was back out of the door and—

'Hoy, Laz, I'll have a hazelnut latte if you're buying.'

Sodding hell.

Too late. He stepped into the canteen. 'Any luck tracking down John Skinner's kids?'

She took another bite of Curly Wurly, chewing with her mouth open. 'Trust me, if there was you'd have heard about it. I'd be running through the station, bare-arse naked singing "Henry the Horny Hedgehog" at the top of my lungs.'

A shudder riffled its way across Logan's shoulders. 'Gah…'

'Oh like *you're* a sodding catwalk model. Least I'm getting some, unlike you. Surprised your right arm's no' like Popeye's by now.' Her teeth ripped a chunk off the twisted chocolate. 'And while we're on the subject, where the sodding hell have you been? Got missing kids to find, remember?'

He stared at her. 'It's *your* case. You took it over, *remember*?'

'Don't be so—'

'And for your information, we've got enough on our plate as it is. Spent half the morning dealing with a sudden death.' He bared his teeth. 'So forgive me if I'm not available to run about after you all day.'

Steel leaned back in her chair and waved her Curly Wurly at him. 'Oh aye, I heard all about your "sudden death". Two missing kids trumps one dead tramp.' The Curly Wurly jabbed towards the canteen counter. 'Now backside in gear, and tell them no' to skimp on the chocolate sprinkles this time.'

Typical.

He got a coffee for himself, and Steel's hazelnut latte. Brought them both back to the table. 'I've spat in yours.'

'No you didn't.' She took a sip. Sighed. 'Got two dozen bodies manning the phones. Heidi and Toby Skinner have

89

been spotted everywhere from Thurso to the Costa del Sol, via Peebles and Chipping Norton.' The creases between her eyebrows deepened. 'Getting a bad feeling about this one, Laz.'

'Just because we haven't found them yet, doesn't mean we won't.'

'When are we ever that lucky?' Steel sank back in her seat and scrubbed her face with her palms, pulling it about like pasty plasticene. Then let her arms drop. 'In other news: tomorrow night. You and Jasmine, daddy–daughter time, with *Despicable Me* one and two.'

'No.'

'You're no' watching a Disney film, Laz: I know you get aroused by all those princesses in their pretty dresses.'

'I'm not being your unpaid babysitter.'

'Come on: it's our *anniversary*.' Steel nudged the parcel with her toe. 'Got Susan the perfect gift. Want to know what it is?'

He glanced beneath the table. Large, rectangular, with a website address printed on the delivery label. 'Something you've ordered off the internet? Nah, I'd rather not know.' It was bound to be something filthy. Probably battery operated.

'You're no fun.' She unwrapped the last inch of twirly toffee and jammed it in her mouth. 'Tell you what: ten quid, *cash*. And a pizza. Can't say fairer than that.'

'No.'

'OK: ten quid, a pizza, and a bottle of red…' She narrowed her mouth to a little pale slit. 'Uh-ho. Crucifixes at the ready, Laz, here comes Nosferatu Junior.'

Logan turned and peered over his shoulder. Superintendent Young was marching across the green terrazzo floor towards their table. Dressed all in black, with a silver crown on each epaulette attached to his black T-shirt. The fabric stretched tight across his barrel chest.

Steel hissed. Then stared at the tabletop, keeping her voice low. '*Don't* move. Don't make eye contact. Don't even *breathe*. He'll get confused and walk away.' She took a deep breath.

Young stopped at the head of the table. 'Inspector. Chief Inspector.'

She didn't move.

Logan nodded. 'Superintendent.'

He pulled up a chair. 'Mrs Black has made another complaint.'

What a surprise. 'Let me guess – Wheezy and I are corrupt because we didn't arrest Justin Robson this morning?'

'Apparently he's bribed you with drugs and dirty magazines. He…' A frown. 'Why is Chief Inspector Steel going purple?'

'Because she's not right in the head.' Logan took a sip of coffee. 'And for the record, there was nothing we could do. Robson killed Mrs Black's parakeets – no doubt about that – but he burned all the evidence. Even his shoes.'

'I see. And is DCI Steel planning on holding her breath till she passes out?'

'Probably. Look, we can't arrest Robson, because we've got nothing on him that'll stand up in court. I've sent the dead parakeets off to the labs, but you know what the budget's like. Assuming we can even get past the backlog.'

'But you're not hopeful, are…' A sigh. Then Young leaned over and poked Steel hard in the ribs. 'Breathe, you idiot.'

Air exploded out of her, then she grabbed the table and hauled in a deep shuddering breath. 'Aaaaaa…'

'I understand you could've arrested the pair of them last night, but didn't.'

'Oooh, the world's gone all swimmy…'

Logan twisted the coffee cup in his hands. 'We felt it was more appropriate to try and defuse the situation with a warning.'

'But Mr Robson didn't take it.'

'Not so much.' A shrug. 'Mrs Black poured paint all over his car and carved "Drug Dealer" into the doors. Probably have to get it completely resprayed. Going to cost him, what – three, maybe four grand?'

Steel blinked. Shook her head. 'Wow. That's a hell of a lot cheaper than a bottle of chardonnay.'

'And in light of this morning's actions?'

Logan raised one hand and rocked it from side to side. 'The aggravated assault and vandalism got no-crimed. I doubt the PF would let us go back and do the pair of them retrospectively.'

'Going to try that again.' Steel took another huge breath and scrunched her face up.

Young frowned at her for a while. 'Has she always been this bad?'

'No, she's getting worse.'

He poked her again. 'We've got twelve different news organizations camped outside the front door, do you think you could try acting a bit more like a grown-up?'

She scowled at him. 'Doing everything we can, OK?' She held up a hand, counting the points off on her fingers. 'National appeal in the media. Whole team going through all Heidi and Toby's friends. Posters up at every train station, bus station, airport, and ferry terminal. We did *three* complete door-to-doors where they live. And...' Steel wiggled the one remaining finger. 'Erm ... This little piggy's being held in reserve in case of emergency.'

'Piggies are toes.'

'Whatever.' She put her hand away. 'If you've got any helpful suggestions, I'll take them under consideration.'

Young shifted in his seat.

'Aye, didn't think so.'

He stood, slid his chair back into place. Straightened his

T-shirt. Stuck a huge, warm, scarred hand on Logan's shoulder. 'And make sure you're getting every encounter with Mrs Black on video. I've got the nasty feeling this is going to blow up in our faces.'

DS Rennie popped his coiffured head around Logan's door. His mouth stretched out and down, like someone had stolen his pony. 'Guv, you got a minute?'

Logan shoved the keyboard to one side. 'If it's more interesting than budget projections for the next quarter, I've got dozens of them.'

'Cool.' He stepped into the office and sank into a visitor's chair. Unbuttoned his suit jacket, then pulled out his notebook. 'I spoke to the janitor at Heidi and Toby Skinner's school, and—'

'Going to stop you right there.' Logan held up a hand. 'Don't tell me, tell Steel. She's running the case.'

A shrug. 'Yeah, but she's doing a press conference, and this was sitting on her desk.' He held up a sheet of A4 with, 'OFF BEING A MEDIA TART – ANYTHING COMES UP, TELL DI MCRAE.'

Typical. Couldn't have given the reins to one of her minions, could she? No, of course not. Not when she could make Logan's life more difficult.

'Anyway…' Rennie went back to his notebook. 'So I spoke to the janitor, the professor from Aberdeen Uni who runs the Saturday maths club, and a really camp Geordie who takes the ballet class. All say the same thing: John Skinner picked Heidi and Toby up at midday.'

'Damn it.' Logan frowned at the screen, ignoring the spreadsheet and its irritating little numbers. Skinner picked up the kids. Did he do it before, or after he killed their mother? Did he make them watch? 'What about family and friends?'

Rennie flipped the page. 'Teams been going through them all morning, but no one's seen the kids.'

And John Skinner's car was still missing.

'OK: if you haven't already done it, get a lookout request on Skinner's BMW. Tell traffic and every patrol-car team it's category one. I want it found. Might be something in there that'll tell us what he's done with Heidi and Toby. Make sure the SEB sample any dirt in the footwells – get it off for soil analysis.' He tapped his fingertips along the edge of the desk, frowning at those horrible little numbers. 'Maybe it's parked on a side street somewhere near where he dropped the kids?' After all, that's how they'd found Emma Skinner. Not that it'd done her any good.

'Yes, Guv.' Rennie stood. 'So … you in charge till Steel gets back?'

Logan folded over and banged his head on the desk a couple of times.

'Guv?'

Of course he sodding was.

Because DCI Steel had struck again.

11

'OK, thanks Denise.' Rennie put the phone down.

Logan looked at him. 'Well?'

'Sod all.'

'Pffff...'

The Major Inquiry Team room was a *lot* grander than the manky hole CID had to work out of. New carpet tiles that were all the same colour, swanky new computers that probably didn't run on elastic bands and arthritic hamsters, electronic whiteboards, a colour printer, a fancy coffee machine that took little pods, and ceiling tiles that didn't look as if they'd spent three months on the floor of a dysentery ward.

How the other half lived.

A handful of officers were on the phones, talking in hushed voices and scribbling down notes.

Logan picked up one of the interactive markers and drew a circle on the whiteboard. There was a small lag, then a red circle appeared on the map of Aberdeen that filled the screen, taking in a chunk of the city centre around the casino. 'John Skinner didn't park in the Chapel Street multistorey and walk the length of Union Street to kill himself. He was clarted in blood – someone would've noticed.'

DS Biohazard Bob crossed his arms and poked out his top lip, as if he was trying to sniff it. It wasn't a good look: with his sticky-out ears, bald patch, and single thick hairy eyebrow, he bore more than a passing resemblance to a chimpanzee at the best of times. 'What about the NCP on Virginia Street? It's just round the corner.'

Rennie shook his head. 'The one on Shiprow's closer.'

'Pair of twits. It's the same car park.' Logan drew a red 'X' on the screen. 'Doesn't matter – logbook says it's been searched. No dark-blue BMW M5.'

Biohazard had a scratch. 'There's a council one on Mearns Street, that's pretty close too. Or Union Square?'

'Or…' Rennie pointed at the map. 'What if he had a long coat on? Like a mac, or something. Could cover up the bloodstains and no one would notice. Dump it when he gets onto the roof of the casino.'

'Nah.' Biohazard shook his head. 'We would've found it on the roof.'

'Not if the wind got hold of it. Could be in Norway by now.'

'True.'

Logan took the pen and marked on all the public car parks within a fifteen-minute walk. 'Rennie – get down to the CCTV room and tell them to go over the footage from Saturday. Any route to the casino from any of these car parks. See if they can find John Skinner.'

'Guv.'

'Biohazard – grab some bodies and work your way through the car parks, find that BMW. Start with the closest, work your way out.'

'Guv.'

The pair of them turned and marched off, leaving nothing but a cloying eggy reek behind.

Logan gagged, wafted a hand in front of his face. 'Biohazard!'

Giggling faded away down the corridor.

'That's us done Union Square. Got a dark-blue beamer, but it's not his. I'm … Hold on.' Biohazard Bob's voice went all muffled, barely audible. *'I don't care. You should've gone before we left the station.'* Then he was back. *'Sorry, Guv, logistical problems.'*

Logan drew a red cross on the whiteboard, eliminating Union Square. 'Might as well try College Street multistorey, while you're there. Then hit the Trinity Centre.'

'Guv.'

The MIT office was nearly deserted. A handful of plain-clothes officers were bent over phones, taking sightings from members of the public. A whiteboard by the fancy coffee machine bore a list of possible locations that now stretched from Lerwick to Naples. A woman with bouffant hair and pigeon toes put her phone down, shambled over, and added 'PORT ISAAC' to the roll.

She puffed out her cheeks, then turned to Logan. 'I know they're only trying to help, Guv, but why do they all have to be *nutters*? Oh, here we go.' Her eyebrows climbed up her forehead and she pointed over Logan's shoulder. 'Showtime.'

He turned and there was Steel on one of the large flatscreen TVs. A media liaison officer sat on one side of her, fiddling with his notes and looking uncomfortable. On the other side were an elderly couple: a grey-haired woman and a bald man, both with dark circles beneath watery eyes. The lines in their faces had probably deepened an inch since Saturday.

Officer Bouffant scuffed over to Logan, staring up at the screen. 'Both sets of grandparents wanted to do it, but the boss thought it'd be best to stick to the wife's side of the family. Might be harder to get sympathy with the murdering wee sod's mum and dad there.'

Logan grabbed the remote and turned the sound on.

'… *thank you.*' The media officer shuffled his papers again. Then held out a hand. *'Detective Chief Inspector Roberta Steel.'*

It looked as if she'd had a bash at combing her hair. And failed. *'Heidi and Toby Skinner were picked up by their father from Balmoral Primary School at twelve o'clock on Saturday afternoon. At one forty-five, John Skinner jumped from the roof of the Grosvenor G Casino on Exchequer Row. At some point between twelve o'clock and one forty-five, Emma Skinner – Heidi and Toby's mother – was subjected to a brutal and fatal attack, along with her friend, Brian Williams, at a house in Newburgh Road.'*

At that, the elderly couple sitting next to Steel quivered and wiped away tears.

Officer Bouffant tilted her head. 'We're calling Williams her "friend". Thought it'd be kinder.'

A copy of that morning's *Daily Mail* sat on the desk beside her. 'Mum And Toyboy Lover In Bloodbath Horror'.

'How did that work out for you?'

She picked up the newspaper and dumped it in the bin. Shrugged. 'Well, it was worth a go.'

'… *appealing for any information that will help us locate Heidi and Toby. Did you see John Skinner's dark-blue BMW M5…*'

Then a sigh. 'Wasting our time, aren't we? Fiver says that gets us nothing but more phone calls from nutters.'

'Yup.'

'… *extremely concerned for their wellbeing…*'

Officer Bouffant curled into herself a bit, shoulders rounding. 'You know what? Being in the police would be a great job, if we didn't have to deal with members of the sodding public.'

'Thank you.' The media officer had another shuffle. *'And now Mr and Mrs Prichard would like to read a brief statement.'*

The old man's voice was cracked and raw, trembling with each breath. *'We've already lost so much. Emma was the brightest, most wonderful human being you could ever meet. She lit up every room...'*

'Think they'll get custody of the kids? You know, assuming we find them.' She folded her arms. 'I mean, the court won't give Heidi and Toby to the dad's parents, will they? Not after what *he* did.'

'Haven't you got phones to answer?'

Sigh. 'Yes, Guv.'

'... bring our grandchildren home, safe and sound. Please, if you know anything, if you saw ... their father...' The poor sod couldn't even bring himself to say John Skinner's name. *'... if you know where our grandchildren are...'* He crumpled, both hands covering his face. His wife put her arm around him, tears shining on her cheeks.

Mr Media did some more shuffling. *'Thank you. We will now take questions.'*

A forest of hands shot up.

'Yes?'

'Carol Smith, Aberdeen Examiner. *Why did John Skinner jump off the casino? Did he have a gambling problem?'*

Steel shook her head. *'No' that we know of. The casino has no record of him ever being in the building before. As far as we—'*

Logan killed the sound and left Steel chuntering away to herself in silence.

It was all just for show anyway. The illusion of progress. Yes, someone *might* spot John Skinner's BMW, but it wasn't likely. The only way they were going to get Heidi and Toby back was by working their way through every parking spot in the city, and hoping there was something in Skinner's car that would point the way.

And hope even more that it didn't point to a pair of tiny shallow graves.

His phone buzzed deep inside his pocket, then launched into 'If I Only Had a Brain'. That would be Rennie.

Logan hit the button. 'What have you got?'

'Guv? Think we've found him.'

'There.' The CCTV tech leaned forward and poked the screen. A figure was frozen in the lower left-hand corner, shoulders hunched, long blue raincoat on over what looked like a grey suit. John Skinner.

Logan nodded. 'It's him.'

She spooled the footage backwards, and he reversed onto Union Street, disappearing around the corner of the Athenaeum pub. 'Took a while, but we managed to—'

'Hoy!' The door thumped open and Steel stood on the threshold, with a mug in one hand and a rolled-up newspaper tucked under her arm. 'Who said you sods could start without me?'

And everything had been going so well. 'Thought you were off being a media tart.'

'Did you see me on the telly? I was spectacular. Like a young Helen Mirren.' She thumped the newspaper against his chest. 'Page four.'

Logan opened the *Scottish Sun* to a spread on 'FATHER OF TWO IN MURDER-SUICIDE SPREE' complete with photos of John Skinner, his two victims, and his missing children.

She poked the article. 'See? "The community has been stunned by Skinner's terrible crimes, and now fears for Heidi – seven – and Toby – six – are growing."' A nod. 'Told you: missing kids trumps dead tramp. Think they're going to run a two-page spread on Gordy Taylor choking on his own vomit? Course they're no'.'

He dumped the paper in the bin. 'That doesn't mean we don't—'

'Blah, blah, blah.' Steel leaned on the desk, close enough to brush the tech's hair with an errant boob. 'What are we looking at?'

'John Skinner.' She shuffled an inch sideways, getting away from Steel's chest. 'So, we track him backwards from the casino...' Her fingers clattered across the keyboard and the scene jumped to the security camera at the junction of Union Street and Market Street. John Skinner reversed across the corner of the image, clipping the edge of the box junction before disappearing again.

'Can barely see the wee sod; can you no' follow him properly?'

The CCTV tech shook her head, flinching as her ear made contact. 'If someone does something and we're there, we can follow him from camera to camera. But we can't jump back in time and tilt and pan, can we? You're lucky we got anything at all.'

Logan's phone rang, deep in his pocket. Please don't be Mrs Black, please don't be Mrs Black. But when he checked the display it was only Marjory from Willkie and Oxford, useless solicitors and rubbish estate agents to the stars. Probably calling with another derisory offer from the Moores. Well, she could go to voicemail. Let it ring.

Steel glowered at him. 'You answering that, or do I have to shove it up your bumhole. We're working here.'

Right. He pressed the button to reject the call. 'Sorry.'

'Think so too.' She eased a little closer to the CCTV tech. 'Come on then – where now?'

Another rattle of keys.

'Markies and the Saint Nicholas Centre probably got him on their cameras, but the next time he shows up is here...' A view across School Hill at the traffic lights. Three cars and a bus stopped on one side, a motorcyclist and a transit van on the other. Skinner lurched backwards across the road and into a short granite canyon blocked off by metal bollards. He reversed past the bank and in through the line of glass doors leading into the Bon Accord Centre. Or more

101

properly, out of it – given the way he'd been going in real life.

She poked the screen as the doors shut, swallowing him. 'That's it.'

'That's *it*?'

'Doesn't appear on foot on any of the other CCTV cameras in the area.' A smile put dimples in her cheeks. 'But I found this.'

The screen jumped to a view down Berry Street, where it made a T-junction with the Gallowgate. Bland granite flats on one side, and a bland granite office block on the other side. A dark-blue BMW M5 came down the Gallowgate and paused in the middle of the junction, indicating right. The opposing traffic dribbled away and it turned onto Berry Street.

She hit pause. 'Number plate matches.'

Steel pressed in even closer. 'So what are we saying?'

Logan poked her on the shoulder. 'Get your boob out of the poor woman's ear.' He pointed. 'Down there you've got John Lewis and the Loch Street Car Park. What about the CCTV camera at the corner of St Andrew Street and George Street?'

'Nope. Far as I can tell, he dumps the car in the car park and walks through the Bon Accord Centre.'

Steel smacked her hand down on the desk. 'Saddle the horses, Laz, we've got two wee kids to save!'

12

The patrol car's sirens carved a path through the Monday rush hour. It was still excruciatingly slow though, crawling along under thirty miles an hour till they got to the junction with Berry Street, where John Skinner had turned right. Then the traffic thinned out and Rennie put his foot down, gunning the engine, throwing them hard around the corner and— 'Eeek!' He locked his arms and stamped on the brakes as the back end of a Citroën Espace burst into view. Its 'BABY ON BOARD' sticker loomed huge, getting huger...

They slithered sideways in a juddering rumble of antilock brakes, coming to a halt half on the pavement.

Steel leaned over from the passenger seat and skelped him round the ear. 'What have I told you about no' getting me killed?'

'Pfffff... That was close.'

'Moron.'

The Espace pulled forward up the ramp, apparently unaware that they nearly had an extra three passengers in the back seat, complete with patrol car.

Rennie backed off the pavement and followed them under

the curved blue sign and into the concrete gloom. A wee queue of traffic led up to an automatic barrier, issuing tickets slower than tectonic plates move.

Steel slumped in her seat. 'Gah. Would've been quicker sodding walking.'

Logan's mobile gave its anonymous ringtone. He pulled it out and checked the screen: Marjory from the estate agents again. He stuck the phone back in his pocket, let it go to voicemail.

Finally, Rennie grabbed a ticket from the geological machinery and pulled up onto the first level. Stopped, craning left and right. 'Which way?'

A forest of concrete pillars reached away into the distance, the space between them packed with cars, all washed in the grimy glow of striplights.

Steel jabbed a finger at the tarmac. 'Follow the arrows. Nice and slow. Anyone spots a BMW, they shout.'

'One more time?' Rennie ran his fingers across the top of the steering wheel as their car emerged from the darkness into the evening sunshine. The ramp curled around to the right, then across a short flyover – suspended three storeys above the street below – and they were back on the roof of John Lewis again.

The last gasp of overflow parking was nearly empty. Half a dozen huge, expensive-looking, shiny, four-by-fours stood sentry on the seagull-speckled tarmac, each one parked as far away from the others as possible, in case someone marred their showroom finish.

Could pretty much guarantee that none of them had seen anything more off-road than the potholes on Anderson Drive.

Steel checked her watch. 'Sodding hell.' She sighed. 'He's no' here, is he?'

Logan leaned forward and poked his head between the

front seats. 'What if he looped round the back of the Bon Accord Centre and onto Harriet Street? Parked in there?'

Rennie shook his head. 'Nah: Harriet's one way.'

Ah. 'Still be a lot of wee places you could leave a car round here though. Not legally, but if you've just stabbed your wife and her lover to death, you probably aren't too bothered about that.'

Steel covered her face with her hands and swore for a bit. Then straightened up. 'One last time round the car park, then we try Crooked Lane. Then Charlotte Street. And anywhere else we can think of.' She kicked something in the footwell. 'Buggering hell!'

'… *your news, travel, and weather at seven, with Jackie.*'

'*Thanks, Jimmy. The trial of Professor Richard Marks enters its third day today, with one prosecution witness claiming the psychiatrist sexually assaulted him on eighteen separate occasions…*'

Rennie swung the car around Mounthoolie roundabout. 'Where now?'

'… *at Aberdeen University since 2010…*'

The massive lump of earth and grass slid by the driver's side, easily big enough to hold its own housing scheme. Surprised no one had thought of that yet. Could make a fortune.

Steel slumped against the passenger window. 'Back to the ranch.'

'… *twenty-three counts. Next up: the grandparents of two missing local children issued an appeal today for information. Heidi and Toby Skinner have been missing since their father committed suicide on Saturday…*'

Rennie took the next left, up the Gallowgate. Grey three-storey flats on one side, grey four-storey flats on the other. The grey monolithic lump of Seamount Court towered over the surrounding buildings with its eighteen-storeys of concrete, narrow windows glittering in the sunlight.

'… you, please: we just want our grandchildren back…'

The North East Scotland College building drifted past the driver's side – in yet more shades of grey.

Logan shifted in his seat. 'Maybe he had an accomplice? Maybe he got out at the Bon Accord Centre and someone drove the kids away?'

'Maybe.' Steel raised one shoulder. 'Or maybe he decided the whole family would be better off dead. You know what these scumbags are like – she's shagging around on him, so *everyone* gets to die.' She stared out of the window at the sea of grey buildings. 'You've really managed to cock this one up, haven't you?'

What?

Logan reached forward and poked her on the shoulder. 'How have *I* cocked it up?'

Rennie kept his eyes on the road, mouth shut.

'You should've had a lookout request going on the kids soon as they scraped Skinner off the cobblestones!'

'Really? Because I remember you saying it was all his own fault and Guthrie should head round and try to shag the widow.'

A sniff. A pause. Then Steel raised an eyebrow. 'To be fair, given what she'd been up to with Brian Williams, Sunshine might have been in with a chance, so—'

'And I don't see you showering yourself in glory here. If it wasn't for me, we wouldn't even *be* searching the car parks!'

Steel's eyes narrowed. 'Nobody likes a smart arse.'

Rennie knocked on Logan's door frame. 'Thought you'd have gone home by now.' His hair was back to its usual blond quiffiness, the tie loosened and top button undone. Bags under both eyes.

Logan leaned back in his office chair. 'Could say the same for you.'

A small smile and a shrug. 'Got everyone we can out looking for Skinner's car. Might have to organize a mass search tomorrow. Half of Aberdeen rampaging through the streets, shouting at blue BMWs. Fun. Fun. Fun.'

'The joy of working for Detective Chief Inspector Steel.'

'Tell me about it. Our Donna's less of a hassle, and she's only six months old. Still, at least we don't have to change Steel's nappies.'

'Yet.'

Rennie curled his top lip. 'Shudder.' Then he hooked a thumb over his shoulder, towards the corridor. 'Bunch of us are heading off to Blackfriars. You wanna?'

Logan shut down his computer. 'Tempting, but I've got to check on a nutjob before I go home.'

Violent pink and orange caught the underside of the grey clouds, as the sun sank towards the horizon. Logan tucked the pool car in behind a Mini on the other side of Pitmedden Court.

Across the road, lights shone from Justin Robson's windows, but Mrs Black's house was slipping into darkness. She was probably sitting in there, on her own, mourning her dead parakeets at the bottom of a vodka bottle. Wondering where her life went so badly wrong.

Maybe plotting revenge on her horrible next-door neighbour.

Not that Justin Robson didn't deserve a good stiff kicking for what he'd done. And got away with.

Still, at least they didn't seem to be at each other's throats this evening. That was something. But there was no way it would last. Sooner or later, one of them was going to open fire again.

Logan pulled away from the kerb, heading back towards Divisional Headquarters.

Should've arrested the pair of them when they had the chance.

Logan let himself into the flat. 'Cthulhu? Daddy's home.' He clunked the door shut. Hung up his jacket. Grabbed the last tin of Stella from the fridge. 'Cthulhu?'

She was through in the lounge, stretching on the window-sill – paws out front, bum in the air, tail making a fluffy question mark. A couple of *proops*, a *meep*, then she thunked down on to the laminate floor and padded over to bump her head against his shins.

The answering machine was giving its familiar baleful wink again.

Well it could sodding wait.

He squatted down and scooped Cthulhu up, turning her the wrong way up and blowing raspberries on her fuzzy tummy as she stretched and purred.

'Daddy's had a crappy day.'

More purring.

The answering machine bided its time, glowering.

Might as well get it over with.

He carried Cthulhu over and pressed the button.

'You have five new messages. Message one:' Bleeeeeep.

'Mr McRae? It's Dr Berrisford from Newtonmyre Specialist Care Centre, we've got your application in for a bed for Samantha Mackie in our neurological ward. Normally there's a waiting list of about six months, but we've had a cancellation. Can you call me back please? I'll be here till about eight. Thanks.'

He hit pause and checked his watch, making Cthulhu wriggle. Seven forty-five. Still time. Cthulhu got placed on the arm of the chair while Logan dug out the paperwork from the coffee table's drawer. Flipped through to Dr Berrisford's contact details. And punched the number into the phone.

Listened to it ring.

'Newtonmyre Specialist Care Centre. How can I help you this evening?'

'Can I speak to Dr Berrisford, please? It's Logan McRae.'

'One moment…'

He sank into the couch. Then stood again. Paced to the window and back.

A deep, posh voice purred down the line. *'Ah, Mr McRae, how are you?'*

'You've got an opening for Samantha?'

'That's right. We were holding a bed for someone, but unfortunately they've passed away.'

'That's great…' Logan cleared his throat. 'Sorry, obviously it's not great for them. I just meant—'

'It's OK. I understand. Now, there are a few things we'll need to sort out, to make sure Miss Mackie can get the best care possible. You are aware of our fee structure?'

Right to the chase.

Logan glanced down at the letter, with its columns of eye-watering figures. 'Yes.'

'Excellent. Well, if you can organize the phase-one payment we'll get the ball rolling.'

Phase one cost more than he made in a year.

He forced his voice to stay level. 'When do you need it?'

'Well, normally we'd say straight away – there is a waiting list – but if you need time to sort things out I can probably extend that to two weeks? Any more than that and I'll have to release the bed again.'

Two weeks. Could probably get a second mortgage organized on the flat by then, couldn't he?

Or he could take Wee Hamish Mowat up on his offer. Borrow enough money to pay the care centre's fees till the mortgage came through.

Sweat prickled the back of Logan's neck. Cross that line and there was no going back. No 'plausible deniability'. He'd be in Wee Hamish's pocket, and that would be that.

Logan's eyes widened. Oh crap...

Wee Hamish.

He'd taken an interest in Samantha's care. Said he'd put in a word. What if he'd done more than that? What if he'd *made* the opportunity.

'Mr McRae? Hello?'

'Sorry.' Logan licked his lips. 'Dr Berrisford, the person who died, how did ... Was it...?'

'Pneumonia. She was due to come up from Ninewells Hospital three weeks ago, but there were complications.' A sigh. *'It's often the case with people in long-term unresponsive states. Chest infections are very difficult for them to deal with and, sadly, she was simply too weak to fight this one off.'*

The breath whoomphed out of Logan, leaving him with eyes closed, one hand clasped to his forehead. Thank God for that. At least Wee Hamish didn't have her killed.

'I see. Right. Two weeks.'

'Let me know if that's not going to be possible, though, OK?'

'No, yes. Right. Thanks.'

He listened till the line went dead, then clicked the phone back in its charger.

Two weeks.

Another deep breath. First thing tomorrow – get an appointment with the bank. See what they could do.

Two weeks.

It was as if something huge and heavy was sitting on his chest.

Logan pressed play on the answering machine again.

'Message two:' Bleeeeeep.

'Logan? What exactly *is wrong with you? I'm your mother and I deserve—'*

110

'You can sod off too.' Poke.

'Message deleted. Message three:' Bleeeeeep.

'Guv? It's Rennie. We're in Archie's, where are you?' The sound of singing and cheering drowned him out for a moment. *'... buck naked. Anyway, we're having another couple here, then maybe grabbing a curry. Give us a call, OK?'*

'Message deleted. Message four:' Bleeeeeep.

'Aye, DI McRae? It's Alfie here from Control. Yon horrible wifie Mrs Black's bin on the phone aboot a dozen times, moaning aboot her neighbour. Are you—'

'Message deleted. Message five:' Bleeeeeep.

'Mr McRae, it's Marjory from Willkie and Oxford, Solicitors again. Hello. I've been trying to get in touch about the young man who came round to view the property this afternoon. He loves the flat and he's made an offer...' She left a dramatic pause.

That was the trouble with people these days – too much time spent watching *Who Wants To Be A Millionaire*, and *Celebrity MasterChef*, and *Strictly Come Sodding Dancing*. They couldn't just come out and say something, they had to build it into a big production number.

'Mr Urquhart wants to know if you'll take the property off the market for twenty thousand pounds over the valuation.'

Logan stared at the machine. *'How* much?'

'Anyway, it's nearly five o'clock, so if you want to give me a call back tomorrow morning, we can see how you'd like to proceed. OK. Thanks. Bye.'

Bleeeeeep.

'How much?' He pressed the button to play the message again.

'Mr Urquhart wants to know if you'll take the property off the market for twenty thousand pounds over the valuation.'

Damn right he would.

He played the message three more times. Then kissed

111

Cthulhu on the head, popped her down on the couch, and toasted her with the tin of Stella. 'Daddy's sold the flat!'

God knew it was about time *something* went right.

— every silver lining —

13

'OK, any questions?' Standing at the front of the MIT office, Steel clicked the remote and the screen behind her filled with the photos of Heidi and Toby Skinner.

A hand went up at the back. 'We still looking for live kids, or is it kids' bodies now?'

Steel scowled through the gathered ranks of uniform and plain-clothes officers. 'You looking for a shoe-leather suppository, McHardy? Cos I don't use lubricant.'

He lowered his hand. 'Only asking.'

'Well don't.' She turned to the crowd again. 'Heidi is seven. Toby is six. They're only wee, and we are damn well going to find them while they're still alive. Am I clear?'

A muffled chorus rippled around the room.

'I said: am I sodding clear?'

This time the answer rattled the ceiling tiles. 'Guv, yes, Guv!'

'Better.' She straightened the hem of her shirt, pulling it down and increasing the amount of wrinkly cleavage on view by about an inch. 'Now our beloved Divisional Commander is going to say a few inspirational words.' She jerked her head towards a big man with a baldy head and hands like a gorilla. 'Come on, Tony, fill your boots.'

While Big Tony Campbell was banging on about civic responsibility and the weight of the public's expectations, Logan flicked through the short stack of Post-it notes that had been stuck to his monitor when he got in. All pretty much the same: 'MRS BLACK CALLED AT 21:05 COMPLAINING ABOUT THE NOISE FROM NEXT DOOR (RAP MUSIC).', 'MRS BLACK CALLED AT 21:30 STILL COMPLAINING ABOUT THE NOISE.', 'MRS BLACK CALLED AT 22:05 COMPLAINING ABOUT RAP MUSIC AND SWEARING FROM NEXT DOOR (AGAIN). SOUNDED DRUNK.' The next six were the same – every fifteen to twenty minutes she'd call up to moan about Justin Robson, apparently sounding more and more blootered each time.

Suppose they'd have to go around there again and read them both the riot act.

So much for the ceasefire.

Big Tony Campbell still hadn't finished being motivational: the power to make a difference, serving the community, proving our detractors wrong. Blah, Blah, Blah.

Steel sidled her way around the outside of the room, till she was standing next to Logan.

Keeping most of her mouth clamped shut, she hissed at him out of one side. 'Don't forget – you're on babysitting duty tonight.'

He kept his face front, expressionless.

She sighed. 'OK: a tenner, a pizza, a bottle of red, and a tub of Mackie's.'

Logan didn't move his mouth. 'What kind of pizza?'

'Microwave.'

'Get stuffed.'

Up at the front, Big Tony Campbell came to the end of his speech and held up his hands in blessing. 'Now get out there and find those children. I know you can do it.'

The younger members of the audience launched into a round of applause. That petered out under the withering stares of the older hands. Some embarrassed clearing of throats and shuffling of feet. Then they started drifting out of the MIT office, heading off on their allotted tasks.

Rennie appeared at Steel's shoulder, stifling a yawn. 'All set, Guv. Both lots of grandparents are on their way for the press conference at eight.'

She didn't look at him. 'I *know* when the press conference is.'

'You knew when the last one was, and you were still fifteen minutes late.'

Her lips pursed, wrinkles deepening at the corners as her eyes narrowed. 'Coffee. Milk and two sugars. And a bacon buttie. *Now*, Sergeant.' Soon as he was gone, she tugged at her shirt again. Any further and there'd be bra on show. 'Cheeky wee sod that he is.'

Logan stuck his hands in his pockets. 'Thought you weren't using John Skinner's parents.'

'United front, Laz. We want them kids back. Our beloved Divisional Commander thinks if we stick both sets up there, the public's more likely to help hunt down John Skinner's beamer.'

'OK, well, have you got a team going door-to-door on Newburgh Road, where we found the wife's car?'

She closed one eye and squinted at him. 'Do I look like a complete and utter numpty to you? Course I have.'

'If someone saw John Skinner turn up to murder his wife, maybe they saw someone else in the car? An accomplice.'

'Yeah, I did *actually* think of that. It's no' my first murder, thank you very much.' A sniff, then another shirt tug, revealing a line of black lace. 'Tell you, Laz, that nasty feeling of mine's getting worse.'

'You're not the only one. I— Sodding hell.' His phone was going again, playing that same irritating anonymous ringtone. 'Sorry.' He pulled it out and pressed the button. 'Hello?'

Nothing.

'Hello?'

A woman's voice, thin and trembling. *'Is this ... Are you Sergeant McRae?'*

'Can I help you?'

'It's over.'

OK. He took a couple of steps away and stuck a finger in his other ear. 'Who am I talking to?'

'It's over. It's finally over. I'm free.'

'That's great. Now, who am I speaking to?' The voice was kind of familiar, but not enough to put a name to it. Distorted and distant, as if whoever it was wasn't really there. 'Hello?'

'I'm free.' Then nothing but silence. She'd hung up.

Nutters. The world was full of nutters.

He checked his call history: 01224 area code – didn't help much, that covered nearly everything from Kingswells to Portlethen and all points in between. Including the whole of Aberdeen. He dialled the number back. Listened to it ring. And ring. And ring. And ring. More soup. And ring...

'Hi, this is Justin's answering machine. I'm afraid he's too busy to come to the phone right now, but you know what to do when you hear the...' Followed by a long *bleeeeeep*.

'Hello? Anyone there? Hello?' Nothing. 'Hello?' Silence. Logan hung up. Frowned down at his phone: Justin.

But it had been a *woman's* voice he'd heard: *It's over. It's finally over. I'm free.*

Logan's eyes widened: *Justin.*

Sodding hell.

He ran for the door.

Grey houses streaked by the pool car's windows. The siren wailed, lights flashing, parting the early morning traffic as Logan tore up Union Street doing fifty. 'Call Control –

whoever's closest, I want a safe-and-well check on Justin Robson. Grade one!'

Sitting in the passenger seat, Wheezy Doug dug out his mobile and dialled. Braced himself with his other hand as the pool car jinked around a bendy bus. 'Control from Sierra Charlie Six, I need a safe-and-well check...'

The Music Hall flashed by on the right, pedestrians stopping on the pavement to gawp as the car screamed past.

'... Justin Robson. ... No, Robson: Romeo – Oscar – Bravo – Sierra – Oscar – November. ... Yes, *Robson*.'

Shops and traffic blurred past. Across the box junction by the old Capitol Cinema.

'Don't care, Control, as long as they get there *now*. We're en route.'

A hard left onto Holburn Street. A van driver's eyes bulged as he wrenched his Transit up onto the kerb. Silly sod should've been on his own side of the road in the first place. The needle crept up to sixty.

'OK.' Wheezy pinned the mobile to his chest, covering the mouthpiece. 'Control want to know what are they sending a car into?'

'Something horrible. Now tell them to get their backsides in gear!'

'Guv.' And he was back on the phone again.

The needle hit sixty-five.

Logan abandoned the Vauxhall sideways across the road, behind a patrol car, and bolted for Justin Robson's house. The front door was wide open, raised voices coming from inside: *'I don't care what they're doing, tell the Scenes Examination Branch to get their backsides over here.'*

He battered into the hall. 'Hello?'

A uniformed officer appeared in the kitchen doorway, hair scraped back, tattoos poking out from the sleeves of her police-issue T-shirt. She had her Airwave up to her ear. 'OK, make sure they do.' Then she twisted it back onto one of the clips on her stabproof vest and nodded at him. 'Sir.' Her mouth turned down at the edges. 'Sorry.'

Logan jogged to a halt. 'Is he…?'

She jerked her head back and to the side. 'Through there.' Then stood back to let Logan in.

Justin Robson's immaculate kitchen wasn't immaculate any more. Bright scarlet smeared the granite worktops. More on the big American fridge freezer. More on the walls. A few drops on the ceiling.

Robson sat on the tiled floor, with his back against one of the units. Legs at twenty-five to four. One arm curled in his lap, palm up, fingers out, the other loose and twisted at his side. Head back, mouth open, eyes staring at the rack lighting. Skin pale as skimmed milk.

He was dressed for work: brand-new trainers, blue jeans, shirt, and tie. Everything between his neck and his knees was stained dark, dark crimson. One of his own huge, and probably very expensive, kitchen knives stuck out of his chest, buried at least halfway in. It wasn't the only wound – his torso was covered with them.

The PC eased into the room and stood well back from the spatter marks with her arms folded. Staring down at the body. 'He's still warm. I've called an ambulance, but *look* at him. Has to be stabbed at least thirty, forty times? No pulse.'

Logan cleared his throat. 'Where's Marion Black?'

She was in the living room, sitting on Justin Robson's couch. Red and brown streaks covered both arms, the black leather seat beside her clarty with more blood. Her tartan jimjams were frayed at the cuffs, the front spattered and smeared.

Logan beckoned the PC over. 'Your body-worn video working?'

She tapped the credit-card-style cover. 'Already running.'

'Good. Stay there.' He stepped in front of Mrs Black – where the BWV would catch them both. 'You phoned me.'

She looked up and smiled. Slow and happy. Peaceful. Like her voice. 'Isn't it lovely and *quiet*?' Her pupils were huge and dark, shiny as buttons.

'Mrs Black, Justin Robson's dead.'

'I know, isn't it wonderful? He's dead and gone and it's all lovely and quiet.' Her fingers made tacky sticky noises on the leather couch. 'He killed my babies and then...' A frown. 'That horrible music at all hours. Pounding away through the walls. Boom, boom, boom...'

'Mrs Black, what—'

'I asked him to turn it down, and he laughed in my face. He killed my babies, and laughed at me. Played that horrible music till I couldn't...' She looked down at her blood-smeared fingers. The nails were almost black. 'And now he's dead and it's lovely and quiet again. We can all live happily ever after.'

'I'm going to need you to come with me.'

She waved a hand at the huge flatscreen TV and the games consoles. 'Why would a grown man need all this stuff?'

'Marion Black, I am detaining you under Section Fourteen of the Criminal Procedure – Scotland – Act 1995, because I suspect you of having committed an offence punishable by imprisonment: namely the murder by stabbing of Justin Robson.'

'It's pathetic, isn't it? All this stuff. All that money. And what good did it do him?'

'You are not obliged to say anything, but anything you do say will be noted down and may be used in evidence. Stand up, please.'

She unfolded herself from the couch. Rubbed each thumb along the tips of her filthy fingers. Caught, literally, red-handed. A frown. 'I'm glad he's dead.' Then the smile was back. 'Now I can sleep.'

14

Steel stood on her tiptoes and peered over Logan's shoulder into the interview room. 'She cop to it?'

'Yes and no.' He eased the door closed, leaving Mrs Black alone with DS Baird and the PC from the house. 'We've got her on BWV admitting she killed him, but in there? She "can't remember". She's "confused". And now she's decided she *does* want a lawyer after all.'

'Gah...' Steel's face soured. 'Want to bet whatever slimy git she gets will tell her to no comment all day, then aim for a diminished responsibility in court tomorrow morning?' Steel went in for a dig at an underwire. 'No' saying I wouldn't buy it, mind. She's off her sodding rocker.'

'She's off her face too. Had pupils the size of doorknobs when we picked her up.' Which was kind of ironic, given her obsession with Robson being a drug dealer. 'Odds on it's antidepressants.'

'Five quid says she cops a plea, gets three or four years in a secure psychiatric facility. Out in two.'

'Ever wonder why we bother?' He tucked the manila folder under his arm and started down the corridor. 'What's the news with Heidi and Toby Skinner? Search turn up anything?'

'Maybe we could get someone to section her? Indefinitely detained in a nice squishy room with a cardie that buckles up the back.'

'He must've parked that damn car somewhere.'

Steel gave up on the underwire and had a dig at the bit in the middle instead. 'Can't be hard getting a shrink to say she's a danger to herself and others, can it? No' with three pints of Justin Robson's blood caked under her fingernails.'

'I was thinking – the big car parks have ANPR systems, don't they? In case you do a runner without paying, they can track you through your number plate.'

'We could get your mate Goulding to section her, assuming he's finished stuffing Professor Marks like a sock puppet. Pervy wee sod that he is.'

Logan frowned. 'Goulding or Marks?'

'Bit of both.' She blew out a breath and sagged against the corridor wall. 'You want to know what we've got on the hunt for Skinner's kids? Sod all, *that's* what. Even with a massive search, there's no sign of the car anywhere. No one's seen it or the kids.' She covered her face with her hands, fingertips rubbing away at her temples. 'McHardy was right – they're dead, aren't they? Don't get them in the first twenty-four hours: they're dead. And it's been three days.'

'We'll find them. And we'll find them *alive*. All we need's one—'

A clipped voice cut through the corridor: 'Ah, *there* you are.' A cold smile followed the words, attached to an utter bastard in Police ninja black. Chief Superintendent Napier. His brogues were polished to dark mirrors, one pip and a crown glowing on his epaulettes. His hair glowed too, a fiery ginger that caught the overhead lighting like a Tesla coil. Napier spread his hands. 'And if it isn't Acting Detective Inspector McRae as well. Just the officers I need to talk to.'

Oh great.

Steel took a deep breath and held it.

Logan poked her. 'If it didn't work on the apprentice, it's not going to work on the Sith Lord, is it?'

A frown creased Napier's forehead. 'Sith…?'

She puffed out the air. 'This about Justin Robson?'

The smile widened and chilled. 'Indeed it is, Chief Inspector. Tell you what, why don't we start with you, and then move on to Acting Detective Inspector McRae? Call it privilege of rank.'

Some privilege. But Logan wasn't about to volunteer to go first.

He backed away down the corridor. 'Right. I'd … better get on with that investigation, then.'

Nice and slow to the corner, then run for it.

Logan wandered up the pavement, away from the knot of smokers kippering each other outside the Bon Accord Centre's George Street entrance. The ribbed, concrete, Seventies lump of John Lewis squatted in the sunlight like a big grey wart, facing off against a row of charity shops, a supermarket, and a pawnbroker's with ideas above its station.

He stuck a finger in his other ear, to shut out the wails of a passing toddler. 'You're sure? *Twenty* grand?'

'I know, it's marvellous, isn't it? He's starting a property portfolio and thinks your flat's an excellent rental prospect. And the offer's unconditional. He's paying cash: we don't even need to do another Home Report!' Marjory sounded as if she was about to pop the champagne. Eighteen months on the market, and it was going for twenty thousand over the asking price. Willkie and Oxford would probably give her a badge. And a hat. *'So, shall I tell him…?'*

'It's a deal.' An extra twenty grand would make a *huge* amount of difference.

'*Wonderful. I'll get the paperwork drawn up and pop it in the post—*'

'Actually, I can probably nip by and sign it. Get the ball rolling.' Before Mr Property Portfolio changed his mind. Or sobered up.

'*Even better. Should be ready for you by lunchtime. We can—*'

Logan walked away a couple of paces and lowered his voice. 'What about the moving date?'

'*Well, standard terms are four weeks, but we can probably stretch that to a month and a half if you need time to—*'

'No, I mean does it have to be that long? Can we make it a week, or ten days, or something?' Ten days – it'd be cutting it close, but at least he'd be able to afford the phase-one payment for Samantha's place at the care centre.

'*Well, it's unusual, but I can try.*'

'Please.' Logan waited till she'd hung up, then had a quick look around to make sure no one was watching before doing a little happy dance. Straightened his tie. Wandered back to the entrance and nodded at DS Baird. 'We good?'

She had one last sook on her cigarette, then nipped the end out and dumped it in the bin. 'Ahhh … I needed that.'

Logan pointed over her shoulder. 'Let me guess, Wheezy?'

Wheezy Doug paced the pavement in front of John Lewis, on his phone, head down, brow furrowed.

'Not this time.' She shook her head, then dug in a pocket for a packet of mints. 'Police Constable Allan "Sunshine" Guthrie. Got stuck with him for three hours this morning. I swear to God, Guv, if I hear the story of how he had a threesome with the cast of *Snow White* one more time, I'm going to kill him.'

'Understandable.'

Baird shuddered. 'I mean, can you imagine it?'

'Rather not.'

Wheezy Doug got to the end of the kerb and stopped,

head bowed over his phone, eyes screwed up. Then there was swearing and coughing. A gobbet of phlegm hit the gutter.

Baird shook her head. 'It's a miracle he's not been invalided out yet.'

Logan stuck his hands in his pockets. 'Steel thinks the kids are dead. We're looking for bodies.'

'Probably. You know what these selfish wee gits are like. Kills the wife, kills the kids, kills himself. If he's going to die, the rest of them have to too.' Her top lip curled. 'How could they *possibly* live without him?'

Wheezy stuffed his phone back in his pocket and lurched over, wiping his mouth with the back of his hand. Eyebrows down. Shoulders hunched. Hands curled into fists. 'Sodding goat-buggering hell.'

Baird grinned at him. 'Good news?'

'Postmortem result on Gordy Taylor. Pathologist says he'd scoofed down about a litre of rough whisky before he died: stomach was sloshing with it. Official cause of death is asphyxia caused by aspiration of regurgitated particulates.'

'Choked on his own vomit.'

'We knew that yesterday.' Logan folded his arms. 'So why all the swearing?'

'Lab's got a new piece of kit in, so they rushed through the tox report as an excuse to play with it. Gordy's blood was full of sleeping pills, painkillers, and ...' he checked his notebook then took his time pronouncing the word in little chunks, 'bro-ma-dio-lone.'

'What's that when it's at home?'

'It's a fancy way of saying "rat poison".'

The smile died on Baird's face. 'Poor Gordy.'

'According to the labs, it was probably soaked into whole grain wheat: you know the stuff they sell in tubs coloured bright blue? You use it to bait traps. Only Gordy didn't have any wheat in his stomach, or in the puddle of vomit he was lying in.'

'That's all we need.' Logan let his head fall back and stared at the sky for a beat. A breath hissed out of him. The other stuff – the drugs – that was easy enough to explain. Gordy breaks into someone's house, raids their medicine cupboard, decides he fancies getting high on whatever he finds, it doesn't react well with the booze, he throws up and dies. But rat poison?

And what had Logan done when the poor sod had been hit by a car and assaulted? Blamed him for being a drunken idiot. Told him it was basically his own fault.

Wonderful: more guilt.

Logan squeezed it down with all the rest. 'Any ideas?'

Wheezy spluttered a bit. Then spat. 'Lab says if you dumped the rat bait in milk, water, or alcohol, you could leach the bromadiolone *out* of the poisoned wheat. And as his stomach was full of whisky…'

'So he drinks a bottle of supermarket McTurpentine laced with rat poison and dies.'

'Nope. Apparently, it takes a day, day and a half for bromadiolone to kick in. It thins the blood and causes internal bleeding – he'd have popped like a water balloon during the postmortem.'

Baird nodded. 'So whoever did it didn't know it'd take thirty-six hours. I mean, it's not suicide, is it? You don't kill yourself with rat poison, you kill other people.'

'Doesn't matter if he choked on his own vomit or not, he would've been dead by Wednesday anyway.' Wheezy's shoulders slumped an inch. 'Suppose it's not my problem any more then. Have to hand it over to the Major Investigation Team.'

Logan patted him on the shoulder. 'Welcome to Police Scotland.'

'Sod Police Scotland. I miss Grampian Police.'

'Better head back to the ranch and get the paperwork started.'

A sigh. 'Guv.' Then Wheezy slouched off.

Baird screwed up one side of her face. 'Rat poison.'

'Not our problem any more.' Logan pushed through into the shopping centre.

'Yeah, but still... It's a CID case, *we* should be the ones chasing it down.'

They marched past the juice bar and into one of the atrium spaces, queuing for the escalator behind a group of school-kids in squint uniforms.

'That's the way things work now. Fighting it will get you nothing but ulcers. And possibly a reprimand, so—' Logan's phone launched into 'The Imperial March' as they glided slowly upwards. That would be Steel, calling up to whinge about Napier.

Baird raised an eyebrow and tilted her head at his pocket. 'You going to answer that?'

'Nope.'

'What if it's important? Maybe they've found Skinner's kids?'

As if they could be that lucky. But maybe Baird was right.

He pulled the phone out and hit the button as they hit the top of the escalator. 'What?'

Steel's voice was low and whispery. *'I need you to set off the fire alarm.'*

Typical.

'I'm not setting off the fire alarm.' Logan followed Baird past a couple of shops, then through a bland grey door marked 'Staff Only'.

'Don't be a dick! Had to fake a dose of the squits so I could get away and phone you. Napier's lurking outside the ladies', making sure I don't do a runner. How untrusting is that?'

'I'm in the Bon Accord Centre.' His voice echoed back

129

from the corridor walls. 'Doubt that setting off the fire alarm here's going to help you any.'

'*You rotten sod! This is no time to do your shopping, get your puckered rectum back here and rescue me!*'

A handful of doors sat at the end of the corridor. Baird knocked on the one with 'SECURITY' on it.

'I can't come back, I'm *busy*.'

'*Busy my sharny arse. If you don't get back here right now, I'm—*'

Logan made a grating hissing noise. '… lo? Hello? Whhhhh…' More hissing. '… an you hear me? Hello?'

'*How thick do you think I am?*'

Ah well, it'd been worth a try. 'Look: I can't come back and rescue you, because I'm trying to find your missing kids. We're…'

There was a clunk, the security door opened an inch, and a little old lady in a brown peaked cap peered out. 'Can I help you?'

'Got to go.' Logan hung up and produced his warrant card. 'Police Scotland. We need to see Saturday's ANPR data for the Loch Street car park.'

'Oh.' She squinted at Logan's ID, then nodded. 'Better come in then.' She opened the door wide, revealing a turd-brown uniform with sweetcorn-coloured buttons and piping. 'You looking for anything specific?'

The room was small, lined with television monitors showing multiple views of the shopping centre. People going about their shoppy business, dragging stroppy toddlers and stroppier boyfriends behind them.

Baird took out her notebook. 'Dark-blue BMW M5, parked here sometime before two.' She rattled off the registration number as the old lady sank into a swivel chair and pulled a keyboard over.

Grey fingers flew across the keys. 'Of course, I should

130

really be asking to see a warrant – data protection and all that – but it's my last day on Friday, so sod it.' A line of letters popped up on the screen. 'Here you go. Got it coming in at twelve oh three.'

Logan leaned on the desk. 'When did it leave?'

More lightning keystrokes. 'That's odd...' A frown, then she leaned forward and peered at the screen. Another frown. Then she put her glasses on. 'Oh, no – here we go. Left at three twenty-two.'

Over an hour and a half after John Skinner did his Olympic diving routine onto the cobblestones.

Baird wrote the details down in her notebook. 'We were right – he had an accomplice.'

Logan hooked a thumb at the bank of screens. 'Can you bring up the car park CCTV footage for then?'

The old lady's fingers clattered across the keys again, and half of the monitors filled with concrete, pillars, and cars. 'There you go.'

He flicked from screen to screen. 'Anyone see Skinner's car?'

'Guv?' Baird tapped one in the top left corner of the display. 'That not it there?'

A dark-blue BMW was heading down the ramp to the exit, only it wasn't doing it under its own steam, it was being towed by a truck with 'ABERTOW VEHICLE SERVICES ~ PARKING ENFORCEMENT' stencilled along the side.

You wee beauty.

'Baird?'

'I'm on it.' She pulled out her phone, poked at the screen then held it to her ear as she pushed out of the room. 'Control? I need the number for a local company...'

The door swung shut, leaving Logan alone with the security guard.

She spooled the footage backwards, following the tow

truck from camera to camera. 'So, what's this bloke supposed to have done?'

'Killed himself.'

'Poor wee soul.'

'But he killed his wife and kids first.'

The old lady pouted for a moment, then nodded. 'Well, in that case, however he committed suicide, I hope it bloody well hurt.'

15

Logan marched across the tarmac, mobile to his ear. 'I don't care if she's got an audience with the Queen's proctologist, get her on the phone. Now.'

'Oh dear...' A deep breath from PC Guthrie, then there was a thunk. A scuffing noise. And the crackle of feet hurrying down stairs.

Abertow's vehicle impound yard sat on the edge of the industrial estate in Altens. Rows of confiscated vehicles sat behind high chainlink fencing. Razorwire curled in glinting coils along the top. Big yellow warning signs hung every dozen feet or so, boasting about dirty big dogs patrolling the place. Should have been one about the seagulls too. They screeched and crawed in wheeling hordes, a couple of them squabbling across the top of a Nissan Micra that had been liberally spattered a stinking grey.

'Yeah, some people just couldn't give a toss.' The large man in the orange overalls tucked his hands into his pockets, the added strain threatening to burst the outfit apart at the groin. He pulled his huge round shoulders up towards his ears. Sunlight sparkled off his shaved head. 'It wasn't really parked, more like abandoned. Right in front of the emergency exit too. What if there'd been a fire?' A sniff. 'Doesn't bear thinking about, does it?'

Another thunk from the phone, then three knocks. Guthrie was barely audible. *'He's going to kill me...'*

What sounded like a door opening. Then a cold voice, slightly muffled by distance. *'This better be important, Constable.'* Napier.

Baird snapped on a pair of blue nitrile gloves, then ripped open the evidence bag with John Skinner's keys in it. The plastic fob for the BMW was cracked and stained with blobs of cherry red.

Guthrie cleared his throat. *'Sorry, sir. But I need to get a message to the Chief Inspector. Ma'am? It's DI McRae, says it's urgent.'*

Baird pointed the fob at the car and pressed the button. Nothing happened.

Napier didn't sound impressed. *'Constable, I think you'll find—'*

'Sunshine!' Steel's smoky growl got louder. *'I take back nearly everything I said about that lumpy misshapen head of yours. That for me? Come on then, give.'* A crackle as the phone was handed over.

Baird shook the keys and tried again. Still nothing.

'Detective Chief Inspector I must insist—'

'Don't think I'm no' enjoying our wee chat, sir, but operational priorities and all that.'

Baird gave up on the fob and stuck the key in the lock instead. *Clunk.* The central locking kicked in.

And Steel was full volume. *'Who dares interrupt my meeting with the glorious head of Professional Standards?'*

'It's—'

'What's that? It's an emergency? Dear God... No, don't worry: I'll be right there.' A sigh. Then the sound became muffled, as if she was holding the phone against her chest. *'Sorry, sir,*

much though I'd love to stay and chat, I gotta go. But we'll always have Paris!' The sound of Steel's boots clacking up the corridor, reverberated out of the phone. Making good her escape. *'Laz, what the hell took you so long?'*

'We've found John Skinner's car. He dumped it in the Loch Street car park and it got towed Saturday afternoon.'

'It got towed?' Some swearing rattled down the line. *'You tell those Automatic Number Plate Recognition idiots I'm going to bury my boot in their bumholes right up to the laces. They were supposed to check!'*

Baird ducked into the car and had a rummage in the BMW's footwells.

'Not their fault. The ANPR camera on George Street only gets traffic coming toward it. The tow truck was in the way.'

'Sod... Any clue where he dumped the kids?'

'Searching the car now. We need to get the SEB up here. See if they can pull fingerprints, or fibres, or something. Maybe get some soil off the floormats and wheech it off to Dr Frampton for analysis? See if she can ID where it came from.'

'Gah.' A click, then a sooking sound. *'Going to cost a fortune, but it's two wee kids we're talking about. If the boss wants to moan about budgets he can pucker up and smooch my bumhole.'*

Baird stood upright. Shook her head. 'Sorry, Guv. Loads of bloodstains and empty sweetie wrappers in there, but nothing obvious.'

Back to the phone. 'You hear that?'

'I'll scramble the Smurfs. And—'

'Guv?' A crease appeared between Baird's eyebrows. She pointed at the boot.

'—you to make sure everyone keeps schtum. I don't want—'

Logan squatted down and peered at the boot lid. A scattering of dark-red fingerprints marked the paintwork beneath the dust. A palm print in the middle, where you'd lean on it to slam it shut. He held his hand out. 'Give me the keys.'

'*Keys? What keys? What are you talking about?*'

Baird pulled off one of her gloves and turned it inside out over the BMW's fob, sealing it away. Then handed it over.

'*Laz? What's going on?*'

'Shut up a minute.' He placed his phone on the ground and put the key into the boot lock. Or tried to. There was something in the slot already – a wedge of metal, the end matt and ragged, as if someone had snapped a key off in there.

Making sure it couldn't be opened.

Oh sodding hell...

He looked up at Baird and tried to keep his voice level. 'There'll be a boot release in the car. Hit it.'

She stared at the boot. Then at him. Then the boot again. 'You don't think...' Baird grimaced. Then scrambled around to the driver's side and ducked in. A dull clunk came from the mechanism, but the boot remained firmly shut. 'Anything?'

'Try again.'

'Come on you little...'

Clunk. Clunk. Clunk.

Still nothing.

The big guy in the too tight overalls sniffed. 'Got a crowbar if you need it?'

'Thanks.' Logan picked up the phone as the yard supervisor lumbered off towards a bright-yellow Portakabin festooned with the Abertow logo. 'There's something in the boot.'

'*What?*'

'If I knew that I would have said.'

'*Don't you get snippy with me, you wee—*'

'Here.' Mr Overalls was back, carrying a long black crowbar covered in scars. He offered it to Baird, then hesitated, hand still wrapped around it. 'Here, do I need to see a warrant or something? You know, if you damage the guy's car—'

'He can sue me.' Baird pulled the crowbar out of Mr Overalls's hand. 'Might want to stand back, Guv.'

On the other end of the phone, Steel was shouting at someone to get the Scenes Examination Branch up to Altens ASAP, followed by various invasive rectal threats involving her boot, fist, and a filing cabinet.

Baird wedged the curved end of the crowbar in under the lip of the boot. 'One, two, three.' She humphed her weight down on the end. *Creak. Groan.* A squeal of buckling metal. Then *pop* and the boot lid sprang open.

The crowbar clattered to the tarmac.

Everyone stepped forward and stared down into the boot.

Then the smell hit. Rancid, cloying, sharp. It dug its hooks into the back of Logan's throat, clenched his stomach, curdled in his lungs.

'Oh God.' Mr Overalls slapped a hand over his nose and mouth, staggered off a dozen paces and threw up all over a Peugeot's bonnet.

Two small bodies lay curled on their sides in the BMW's boot. A little boy and a little girl. Heidi and Toby Skinner, barely recognizable. Sunken cheeks, cracked lips, electric cable wrapped around their wrists and ankles. Faces smeared with blood. Still and pale.

Baird chewed on her bottom lip. Looked away. 'You shouldn't have let him jump, Guv. You should've dragged that bastard down from the ledge so we could all kick the living *shite* out of him.'

Poor little sods.

Baird was right.

Logan let out a long shuddering breath. Stood upright. Squared his shoulders. Snapped on a pair of blue nitrile gloves. Cleared his throat. 'Denise, I need you to get on to the Procurator Fiscal. And we'll need the Pathologist. Better get the Duty Doctor out too.'

A nod. But she didn't turn around. 'Guv.'

Two little kids. How could *any* father do that?

Logan reached into the boot. Brushed the hair from little Heidi Skinner's face. Seven years old.

'Guv? You shouldn't touch them. The SEB need to take photos.'

A flicker. There. That was *definitely* a flicker.

You wee beauty!

Logan scooped Heidi out of the boot.

'Guv!' Baird grabbed his sleeve, voice low and hard. 'Have you lost your bloody marbles? The PF—'

'Get the car! Get the sodding car, now!'

16

Logan pulled on his jacket, then poked his head into the CID office. Wheezy Doug was hunched over the photocopier, jabbing at the buttons as if the machine had suggested his mother was romantically intimate with donkeys on a regular basis.

No sign of Stoney. But DS Baird was on the phone, elbows on the desk, one hand pressed to her forehead.

'Uh-huh. ... Yeah. ... OK, well, let me know.' She put the phone back in its cradle and looked up. 'Hospital says Heidi Skinner's responding well to the IV fluids. Just woke up.'

'What about Toby?'

'Heidi's freaking out. Three days, locked in a boot with your brother. In a car parked in the sunshine ... I'd be freaking out too.'

'Denise: what about Toby?'

She puffed out her cheeks. Stared down at the phone. 'He was only six, Guv.'

'Sodding hell.' Something heavy grabbed hold of Logan's ribcage and tried to drag him down to the grubby carpet tiles. A deep breath. Then another one. 'I should've checked the car park's ANPR sooner. I should've done it soon as we found out the car was missing. I should've…' He mashed his teeth together. Clenched his fists. Glowered at the filing cabinet. Then took two quick steps towards it and slammed his boot into the bottom drawer, hard enough to rattle the mugs and kettle balanced on top. Hard enough to dent the metal. Hard enough to really regret it five seconds later as burning glass rippled through his foot. 'Ow…'

'Three days.' Baird slumped further down in her seat. 'It's a miracle she's alive at all. Doctor said any longer and her internal organs would've started shutting down.'

Wheezy jabbed away at the photocopier again. 'Don't know about anyone else, but I'm going to the pub tonight and getting sodding wasted.'

Baird nodded. 'I'm in. Guv?'

Logan turned and limped back towards the door. 'I'll see you there. Got something to sort out first.'

Marjory stood up and held a hand across her desk for shaking. Her smile looked about as real as the potted plant in the corner. 'Mr McRae, I was beginning to think you'd changed your mind.'

Three walls of the office were covered with racks of schedules, complete with photographs of various bungalows, flats, and semidetatched rabbit-hutches in Danestone and Kincorth.

Logan settled into the chair on the other side of the desk. 'Been a rough day.'

'Well, not to worry, there's still time.' She dug into a tray on her desk and came out with a chunk of paperwork. Passed it across to him. 'As you'll see, there are no demands or conditions. They asked for a four-week entry date, but I went back to them with your proposal for ten days and they accepted.' The fake smile intensified. 'Now, if you need help finding a new property in a hurry, we'd be delighted to help you with that. We've got a lot of excellent homes on—'

'I've got something sorted, thanks.' Even if it was a static caravan, equidistant from Aberdeen's worst roundabout, a sewage treatment plant, and a cemetery. At least the chicken factory had moved somewhere else. That was something.

And ten days from now, Samantha would be getting the specialized care she needed. Everything else was just noise.

'Oh. Well, I'm sure you know best.' Marjory handed him a pen. 'If you sign where I've put the stickers, we'll get everything faxed over to Mr Urquhart's solicitors and that's that.'

Logan skimmed the contract, then scrawled his signature where the big pink stickers indicated.

'Excellent.' She took the paperwork back. 'Congratulations, Mr McRae, you've sold your flat.'

It should have been a moment of joy. An excuse to celebrate for a change. But after what happened to poor wee Toby Skinner?

Logan scraped back his chair and stood.

Time to go to the pub. Meet up with the team. And try to drink away the horror of two little bodies, locked in a car boot.

The celebration could wait.

— boxes, bins —

— and dead little bodies —

17

'Gah...' Steel pulled the e-cigarette from her mouth and made a face like a ruptured frog. 'Look at it. Could you no' have picked a better day to move?'

Rain rattled against the kitchen window. Wind howled across the extractor fan outlet – mourning the end of an era.

Logan wrapped a strip of brown parcel tape around the last box. 'Don't know what you're moaning about.' He printed 'BOOKS' across the top in big black-marker-pen letters, then put it with the other two by the front door. 'Not as if you've *actually* been helping.'

'Supervising's helping.'

'Not the way you do it.' Logan stuck the marker back in the pocket of his jeans.

His footsteps echoed from the laminate floor to the bare walls and back again as he checked the bedroom for the final time. Empty. Then the living room. Empty. Then the kitchen. Empty. And the bathroom. Every trace of him was gone – packed away over the last ten days and carted out to the removal van. Nothing but echoes and three packing boxes left to show he was ever there at all.

Steel slouched along behind him. 'You've got OCD, you know that, don't you? Place is cleared out.'

The front door clunked open and Duncan was back. Rain had darkened the shoulders of his brown boilersuit, plastered his curly fringe to his forehead. A smile. 'Nearly done.' He stacked two of the last boxes, hefted them up with a grunt, then headed back down the stairs again.

Logan turned on the spot. One last slow three-sixty.

No point being sentimental about it. It was only a flat. A container to live in. Somewhere to sleep and brood and occasionally drink too much.

Still...

Steel sniffed. Dug her hands into her pockets. Stared off down the corridor. 'Susan says you can always come stay with us for a bit, if you like. Don't have to be trailer trash, down by the jobbie farm.'

Logan grabbed the final box. 'It's a lovely offer. But can you imagine *you* and *me* living together? In the same house? Really?'

'No' without killing each other.'

He pulled a thin smile. 'Thanks though. Means a lot.'

She thumped him on the arm. 'Soppy git.' Then sniffed. 'Well, suppose I better get back to it. Got a rapist to catch.'

Logan followed her out onto the landing, then pulled the door shut with his foot. The Yale lock clunked. And that was it. No more flat.

Steel thumped down the stairs.

Look on the bright side: at least now he could pay for Samantha's care.

Deep breath.

He nodded, then followed her. 'Any closer to catching the scumbag who killed Gordy Taylor?'

'Pfff ... I wish. No' exactly doing my crime figures any good. Nearly a fortnight, and sod all progress.' They got to

146

the bottom and she held the building's front door open. Then screwed up one side of her face. 'Sodding hell. Going to get soaked.'

Rain bounced back from the grey pavement, darkened the granite tenement walls of Marischal Street. Ran in a river down the steep hill, fed by the overflowing gutters.

The removal van was parked right outside, the back door open as Duncan strapped the fridge-freezer to the wall.

Steel stayed where she was, on the threshold just out of the rain. Pulled a face, then dug into her coat and pulled out a copy of that morning's *Aberdeen Examiner*. A picture took up half of the front page – a smart young man, standing to attention, with medals on his chest and a beret on his head. 'War Hero "Let Down By Police" Say Grieving Parents'

She gave it a wee shake as rain drops sank into the news-print. 'Apparently it's *our* fault he ended up dead behind the bins. Well, us and those shiftless sods in Social Services. Oh, and the NHS. Don't want to be greedy and claim *all* the guilt for ourselves.'

'What were we supposed to do?'

'Every morning it's like waking up and going for a sodding smear test.' She produced her phone and poked at the screen with a thumb. 'I've had two reviews, three "consultancy" sessions with a smug git from Tulliallan, supervisory oversight from Finnie *and* Big Tony Campbell, and we're no closer than we were when Gordy turned up dead behind the bins. Rennie's latest theory is we've got a serial killer stalking the streets, knocking off tramps.'

'Well...' A frown. 'He *could* be right, I suppose. Maybe?'

'After a heavy night on the Guinness – with a dodgy kebab, a box of Liquorice Allsorts, and a bag of dried prunes – I'd still trust a fart before I'd trust one of Rennie's theories. My bet? Gordy fell out with one of his mates and they poisoned him.' She hoiked up her trousers. 'That, or the silly sod thought rat poison would be a great way to get high...' Steel frowned at her phone. 'Buggering hell.' She held it out. 'Speaking of DS Useless, look at that.'

Guv. We got anuthr vctim 4U @ Cults.

U cming Ovr??

Wnt me 2 snd U a car??!?

'I swear, his spelling's getting worse.' She thumbed out a reply. 'You sure you don't want me to transfer him back to CID? Be a valuable addition to your team.'

'Bye.' Logan squeezed past her into the rain. Hurried around to the back of the removal van and handed the box of books up to Duncan. 'That's the lot, we're done.'

'Good stuff.' He put it with the others, strapped it into place, then hopped down to the ground and hauled the rolling door shut. 'Right. See you over there.'

Logan stepped back onto the pavement. Gave the van a quick wave as it pulled away from the kerb and grumbled its way up the hill.

Rain seeped into the shoulders of his sweatshirt.

Well, that was that then. Fourteen years in the same flat. A stone's throw from Divisional Headquarters, two bakers, three chip shops, and loads of good pubs. And now he'd have to fight his way around the sodding Haudagain Roundabout at *least* twice a day. Oh joy of joys. It was—

'Mr McRae?'

He turned, and there was Marjory from the solicitors, sheltering beneath a golf umbrella with the firm's name plastered around the outside.

Logan dug into his pocket and came out with the flat's keys. 'Was on my way up to see you.'

She smiled her fake smile. 'That's very kind, but at Willkie and Oxford we want to make everything as easy as possible for you.' She held out her hand, palm up.

Fourteen years.

He passed her the keys.

'Excellent. Thank you.' She turned and waved at an Audi TT, parked a little bit up the hill. 'I'll give these to Mr Urquhart, and we're all done. Congratulations, Mr McRae, I hope you'll be very happy in your new home. And if you ever decide to sell it, I *do* hope you'll think of Willkie and Oxford.' One last go on the smile, then she marched up to the Audi.

The driver buzzed open the window and she bent down, had a brief chat, handed over the keys, shook his hand, then marched off towards Union Street.

Ah well, might as well head over to the caravan and get unpacking.

He unlocked his manky old Renault Clio. Pot plants and picture frames filled the back, but a large cat-carrier sat on the passenger seat – the seatbelt threaded through the handle on the top, bungee cords securing the whole thing into place.

Cthulhu pressed up against the carrier's door and yowled, a pitiful wailing noise that sank its claws in his chest. Her fur poked out through the bars in grey and brown tufts, one paw scratching at the hinge.

'I know, shhh … We'll be in our new home soon, I promise.' He slipped a finger between the bars and stroked her on the head. 'Shhh … it's OK. Daddy's here.'

There was a brief honk, and Logan peered out through the rain-rippled windscreen. The Audi had pulled into the space where the removal van used to be. Its driver grinned and waved at him.

The guy looked familiar. No idea why, though.

Logan gave Cthulhu another stroke. 'Wait here, Daddy will only be a minute.'

He climbed back out into the rain and closed the door on her tortured wails.

Mr Audi stepped out and popped a collapsible brolly up above his head. Expensive-looking black suit, lemon shirt open at the neck, neat brown hair, flashy stainless-steel watch. Couldn't have been much more than twenty, twenty-five tops. Little pockmarks covered both cheeks, the ghosts of acne past. He stuck out his hand. 'Mr McRae, no' seen you for ages, yeah?'

OK…

Logan took the proffered hand and shook it. Tilted his head to one side. Nope, still no idea. 'Mr Urquhart?'

He grinned again, showing off small white teeth separated by little gaps. 'It's the hair, isn't it? Finally grew out of dying it green. You like the suit?' He did a little catwalk two-step. 'Got it made special like.'

Green hair?

No. Couldn't be.

Logan squinted at him. 'Wait a minute. Urquhart. *Jonny* Urquhart?'

'Bingo!' He stuck a thumb up.

Oh sodding hell. No, no, no, no, no…

'You bought my *flat*?'

'Yeah.' He glanced up at the building. 'Cool, isn't it? Starting my own property empire. Mr Mowat says a man's got to put down proper business roots in the community.'

Christ. What if Professional Standards found out?

What if Napier found out he'd sold his flat to someone who worked for Wee Hamish Mowat, Aberdeen's biggest bloody crime lord? And if that wasn't bad enough, that they'd paid twenty thousand pounds over the asking price. *Twenty thousand* sodding pounds.

Logan took a couple steps away, then back again. 'You *can't* buy my flat! What the hell were you thinking?'

Jonny Urquhart's eyebrows went up. 'Eh? Steady on, it's win-win, right?'

'Win-win? WIN-WIN?' He threw his arms out. 'DO YOU HAVE ANY IDEA HOW THIS *LOOKS*?'

'Don't worry: the money's clean. Laundered to a crisp and shiny white.' He placed a hand against his chest, fingers spread, as if he was about to pledge allegiance to something. 'Mr Mowat gives me a bonus for my loyal service. You get your flat sold. And your girlfriend gets to go to a nice private hospital with excellent facilities. Win-win-win.'

'Oh God...'

He was screwed. Completely and utterly *screwed*.

18

First would come the investigation. Then the accusations. Then the recriminations. Prosecution. And eight to twelve years in Glenochil Prison with all the other bribe-taking dodgy police officers.

Oh God.

Logan closed his eyes and let his head fall back against the wall. 'Brilliant.' He gave it a little thump. Then a harder one. 'Sodding – bloody – brilliant.' Banging his head with every word.

Samantha's static caravan had developed its familiar peppery soil-and-dust scent again. The smell of mildew and neglect. Served him right for not coming down here and airing it out more often. Boxes filled the living room and the bedroom. More piled up in the tiny galley kitchen, with the mouse droppings. Green-brown slime growing in the shower cabinet and across the bathroom tiles. A lovely view across the river to the sewage treatment plant.

Welcome home.

But it was better than a cell.

Cthulhu clearly didn't agree. Her cat carrier sat on the

couch, amongst the pot plants, and she glowered out from its depths. Refusing to come out.

Logan let out a long, rattling breath.

Might be a good idea to head over to the B&Q in Bridge of Don and see if they had any anti-mildew paint, maybe a dehumidifier. And something to take away the *smell*.

And maybe just enough rope to hang himself.

'… because we've got hundreds of bargains, bargains, bargains!' Whoever was on the store's PA system, they needed battering over the head with a lump-hammer. Then stuffed in a sack with a couple of breezeblocks and dumped in the River Don. *'There's* massive *savings on tiles and laminate in our flooring department, right now!'*

Logan drifted along the aisle, hunched over his trolley. Phone to his ear, staring down at the three pots of paint, set of brushes, roller, and paint tray in there. 'There's no way? You're sure? I mean, a hundred percent positive?'

On the other end, Marjory sighed again. *'Mr McRae, we've been over this. Missives have been exchanged, money's changed hands. You signed the contract. You've handed over the keys. That's it done.'*

'But … there has to be a loophole, or something. People wriggle out of contracts all the time.' He turned the corner, slouching his trolley past burglar alarms and home CCTV systems. 'I checked with my bank, the cash hasn't come through yet, so he hasn't—'

'Mr Urquhart paid cash: it's in our account. And as we're your legal representatives, the minute that money hit our bank account it's deemed to be paid to you. There's nothing you can do.' A sigh. *'Now, I'm really going to have to go. The money will be in your account, less our fee, as soon as your bank clears our cheque. Goodbye, Mr McRae.'*

And she hung up on him. Unbelievable.

The CCTV systems gave way to locks and bolts. Then padlocks. Then chains and ropes. For all your wholesale bondage-dungeon needs.

Napier was bound to find out.

Then Logan would be screwed.

And probably in for a spanking.

He stopped. Stared at the paint. *Swore*.

It'd take at least three days for the solicitor's cheque to clear. Plus the ten days they'd already taken…

Oh sodding hell. And it was Friday. So the useless greedy sods at the bank wouldn't do anything about it till Monday.

Which would be fifteen days, in total, since Dr Berrisford at Newtonmyre Specialist Care Centre said he'd keep Samantha's bed open for two weeks.

Sodding, buggering, bloody hell.

He pulled out his phone and called Directory Enquiries. Got them to put him through to the centre. Maybe Dr Berrisford would give him a little leeway? He only needed a day. Twenty-four hours. *Surely* they could do that.

The phone rang.

Logan pushed his trolley around the corner, into an aisle lined on either side with hardware. Hammers. Pliers. Screwdrivers.

Still ringing.

A chirpy voice: *'Newtonmyre Specialist Care Centre, how can I help you today?'*

'I need to speak to Dr Berrisford. It's Logan McRae.'

'Oh, I'm sorry, but Dr Berrisford has gone home for the weekend. Would you like to leave a message?'

'Yes. Tell him…' Logan stared at the claw-hammers. 'Tell him I'll put the cheque for phase one in the post tomorrow. You should get it on Monday.' After all, it would take *their* bank three days to clear it as well, wouldn't it?

'That's lovely. You have a good weekend, Mr McRae.'

'You too.' He hung up.

Oh – thank – God. They'd take the cheque, Samantha could go into the care centre, everything would be fine.

All that panic, and there was nothing to worry about.

Clunk.

Logan's trolley jerked in his hand as someone collided into it. He looked up to apologize, even though he'd been standing perfectly still, and froze.

The man was huge, tall and wide, hands like bear-paws wrapped around his trolley's handle. Face a mixture of scar tissue and fat, stitched together by a patchy beard. A nose that was little more than a gristly stump. He pulled on a piranha smile. 'Well, well, well. Look who the cat coughed up.'

Logan swallowed. Stood up straight, shoulders back. 'Reuben.'

He'd lost a bit of weight since last time – but not enough to shrink that massive frame – and ditched his usual grubby overalls for a dark-grey suit. Blood-red shirt. No tie. 'Fancy running into you here. What are the chances, eh?'

Logan didn't move.

'Aye, well, maybe no' such a coincidence after all.' He reached out and plucked a crowbar from the rack beside him. Shifted his grip, then smacked the chunk of metal down into the palm of his other hand. 'What with me following you and everything.'

'Why?'

'See, I don't need to worry about you, do I?' *Smack.* 'Don't need to worry about you at all.' *Smack.*

Don't back off. Don't stare at the crowbar. 'Really.'

Reuben's trolley was stacked with rubble sacks. Duct tape. A bow saw. A hand axe. A box of compost accelerant. And a shovel. The smile graduated from piranha to great white. 'See, if you try to move against me –' *smack*, '– try to take

155

what's *mine* –' *smack*, '– I'm no' gonnae bother ripping your arms and legs off.' *Smack*. 'No' gonnae haul out your teeth and cut off your tongue.' *Smack*. 'Gouge out your eyes. Nah. Don't have to do any of that.'

There was something worse?

Reuben winked. 'All I've got to do, is clype.'

Something dark spread its claws through Logan's chest. 'Clype?'

'Oh aye.' He placed the crowbar in his trolley. 'What, you think Jonny came up with the idea to buy your flat all on his *own*?' A laugh barked out of that scar-ringed mouth. 'Nah. See, some people think I'm thick. Think I'm all about the violence and no' so much the brainpower. The planning. Nah.'

Oh sodding hell. Sodding, *buggering* hell.

The claws dug in deeper.

'See, McRae, I own you. Get in my way and I'll squash you like a baby's skull. When Mr Mowat passes, I'm stepping up. And then we can talk about what kinda favours you're gonnae do me to stay out of jail.' One last wink, then Reuben walked his trolley past. Whistling *The Dam Busters* theme tune.

Something happened to Logan's knees. They didn't want to hold him upright any more.

Reuben knew. *Reuben*.

No, no, no…

Oh God.

He rested his chest against the trolley's handlebar. Let it take the weight for a bit. Closed his eyes.

Agh…

Think.

There had to be a way out of this.

OK, so he couldn't break the contract. At least there was a chance of proving that he'd *tried* to. Get Marjory from

Willkie and Oxford up on the stand and question her under oath. *'Yes, Mr McRae tried to weasel his way out of the contract.'* That would help, wouldn't it?

Might cut a year or two off his sentence...

Oh God.

Why did it have to be *Reuben*?

He was completely and utterly screwed.

A woman's voice: 'Are you OK?'

Deep breath.

Logan blinked a couple of times. Straightened up. 'Sorry. Having a bit of a day.'

She was tiny, with long red hair and round freckled cheeks. According to the name badge pinned to her bright-orange apron, this was Stacey. Stacey smiled at him. 'Anything I can help you with?'

He sighed. Pulled out the envelope he'd jotted everything down on and frowned at it. 'Mildew, damp stuff, paint, mice, and something to clean grout with.' He held the list out.

'Right, OK. Well, we can cross out "paint". Is your damp coming through a wall, or is it condensation?'

'Condensation. Probably. Maybe.'

'Right, follow me then!' She led the way, down to the end of the aisles, then over another two.

Maybe he *should* take Wee Hamish up on his offer after all? If Reuben was face down in a shallow grave, he couldn't tell anyone, could he? Or better yet – fed to the pigs. They wouldn't care how ugly he was, they'd chomp through flesh and bone, leaving nothing but Reuben's teeth behind.

Stacey came to a halt, and swept a hand up. 'Here we go.' The shelves were filled with bottles, jars, sprays, and tubs, beneath a sign marked 'DAMP, MOULD, AND MILDEW CONTROL'.

She scanned the rows of products. 'You're going to need some of this...' She hefted a ten-litre pot of anti-mould paint into the trolley. Added a second one. 'Just in case. Nothing worse than getting halfway through a job and having to come back.'

Mind you, might be a better idea to go DIY with Reuben too. The more people who knew, the more chance of getting caught. Wee Hamish wasn't going to kill his right-hand man himself, was he? In the old days, maybe. But now? Lying on his back, wired up to drips and monitors, being devoured by cancer? He'd have to farm it out.

Stacey grabbed half a dozen plastic tubs containing silica gel that promised to suck moisture out of the atmosphere. 'You want to keep these in the cupboards where the mildew is.' She checked the list again. 'Right: grout cleaner.'

Maybe he should head back and pick up a crowbar of his own? Or a lump hammer. Something to crack Reuben's head open with. Too risky trying to get his hands on a gun...

Who was he trying to kid?

He couldn't kill Reuben. Couldn't.

That hollowed him out, left him standing there in the middle of B&Q, with a hole in his chest the size of a water-melon.

He was going to prison...

Oh God.

Stacey teetered down the aisle a bit and plucked a spray bottle from a shelf. 'That should help. So I think that leaves "mice", right? You want to keep them as pets, or get rid of them?'

'Rid.' Then again, why bother? Why do up a manky static caravan, when he was going to spend the next eight years in a cell anyway?

'Follow me.'

Two aisles along she stopped and pointed. 'We've got humane traps, normal traps, and *in*humane traps.' She picked up a couple of plastic things that looked as if they could take a finger off. 'These are pretty much instant death, so the mouse won't suffer much.'

Lucky mice. A quick and painless death…

Might not be a bad idea. He could jump off something tall, like John Skinner. Ten storeys, straight down. Goodbye cruel world. Splat.

'These are the humane ones.' She held up what looked like a small, bent, rectangular telescope. 'They get stuck inside, and can't get out. Then you drive at least four miles away and release them into the wild.' Her mouth turned down at the ends. 'Or you could go inhumane and poison them.' She poked a box marked 'BAIT STATION BRAVO!' with a finger.

Sitting next to it was a tub with a red lid and a warning sticker across the top and 'BROMADIOLONE-TREATED WHOLE WHEAT' down the side.

Rat poison.

Logan picked it off the shelf. Turned it over in his hands. The contents hissed against the plastic innards.

'My bet? Gordy fell out with one of his mates and they poisoned him.'

No chance. What, someone living on the streets marched into B&Q, bought themselves a thirty-quid tub of this stuff, then a litre of whisky, mixed them together and let them sit till the poison was all leached out, put it back in the bottle, and gave it to Gordy Taylor as a gift? Why not drink the whisky yourself and batter his head in with the empty bottle? Why go to all that trouble?

'Rennie's latest theory is we've got a serial killer stalking the streets, knocking off tramps.'

Yeah, but Rennie was an idiot.

But there *was* something a lot more likely. What if—

'Hello? Excuse me?' Stacey was tugging at his sleeve.

Logan blinked at her. 'Sorry, miles away.'

She shook her head. 'You've got a cat, haven't you? I can tell by the hairs all over your jeans.' Stacey looked up at him, still holding on to his arm. 'If it was me, if I had a cat, I wouldn't want poisoned mice staggering around the house looking to get caught and eaten. Would you?'

'Ah...' He slid the tub back onto the shelf. 'No.'

Then stopped, fingertips just touching the label.

Poisoned mice staggering around.

All you have to do is put the stuff where they can find it. They eat it, because it's in their nature to eat whatever they can get their paws on. It's what mice do. Make the poison tasty enough and they'll do all the hard work for you...

Stacey tugged at his sleeve again. 'Are you sure you're OK?'

Logan grabbed four of the finger-snappers. 'Thanks for your help: gotta go.' Then marched the trolley away to the tills.

'*Guv?*' Wheezy paused for a cough. '*Thought you were having a day off.*'

The Clio crawled along the Parkway, around the back of Danestone in the rain. Fields on one side, identikit houses on the other, with a long slow-moving clot of rush-hour traffic in-between.

It was only four thirty-five. All these sods should still have been at work instead of clogging up the bloody roads.

Logan switched the phone to his other ear and put the car in gear again. Easing forward another six feet as the windscreen wipers groaned across the glass. 'When we did the door-to-doors on Harlaw Road, did you check everyone's alibis?'

'*Guv?*'

'When Gordy Taylor died. We questioned all the residents

– did someone chase up the alibis? Was everyone where they said they were?' A gap had opened up in front of the Nissan he was grinding along behind – had to be at least three car-lengths and the silly sod in front still hadn't moved. Logan leaned on the horn. 'COME ON, GRANDAD!'

'But…'

'Not you, Wheezy, this pillock in front.'

'It wasn't a murder when we were in charge, it was a sudden death. There wasn't any reason to check. Then the MIT took it over.'

The Nissan finally got its bum in gear and they all inched forward a bit.

'What about Steel's team then, did they check alibis?'

'Er, hold on.' There was some clunking and rattling. The cars drifted forward another two lengths. Rustling. A thump. Then the sound of fingers punishing a keyboard, and Wheezy was back. *'Right. According to the system, pretty much everyone was home that night. A couple families were at the cinema, two went to the theatre, and one guy was on a works night out. Looks like the MIT followed up and everything checked out. Why?'*

'Thinking.' Logan tapped the fingers of his free hand along the top of the steering wheel. 'What if DCI Steel's right, and Gordy *did* poison himself? Just not on purpose. He thinks his ship's come in – a whole litre of whisky, all to himself. So he crawls off behind the bins and swigs it down. But he doesn't know it's laced with bromadiolone.'

Someone behind leaned on their horn, and Logan looked up to see a four car-length gap between himself and the Nissan in front. Another *bleeeeeeeeeep*.

Impatient git.

Logan eased forward into the space. 'Did you get any prints off the bottle?'

'What bottle?'

'The bottle of whisky Gordy drank: did you get finger-prints?'

161

'There wasn't one. Don't think so, anyway.' The rattle of fingers on a keyboard sounded in the background. *'Nothing got signed into evidence.'*

They'd finally reached the corner where the Parkway turned downhill towards the Persley roundabout. The traffic snaked away in a solid ribbon ahead, trapped single-file by the double white lines protecting the overtaking lane on the other side of the road. And once he'd managed to fight his way through all this, there would be the Haudagain. And then Anderson Drive to traverse. At rush hour. It would take hours.

Maybe not though.

A patrol car was coming the other way, up the hill. He flashed his lights at it, leaned on his horn … but they drove right past. Didn't even clock him on his mobile phone. Lazy sods.

'Wheezy, I need you to get onto Control, tell them…'

Blue lights flickered in his rearview mirror. The patrol car was doing a three-point turn.

'Guv?'

'Never mind. Meet me where they found the body, and make sure you bring some photos of Gordy Taylor with you.'

The patrol car pulled up alongside, lights flickering. The officer in the passenger seat wound down his window. 'Sir, do you know it's an offence to use your mobile phone while—'

'Murder enquiry.' Logan flashed his warrant card. 'Get the blues-and-twos on. You're escorting me to Harlaw Road.' Nothing happened. '*Now*, Constable.'

The officer blinked a couple of times. 'Yes, Guv.'

And they were off: siren roaring, lights blazing, carving a path through the oncoming traffic with Logan's manky old Clio puttering along behind.

19

'And they searched all round here?' Logan pointed at the bushes behind and on either side of the council's communal bins.

Wheezy nodded, rain drumming on the skin of his black umbrella. 'Far as I know. Got a couple of condoms and some litter, but that was it.'

No empty whisky bottle.

Harlaw Road huddled beneath the slate-grey sky, all the colours muted by the downpour. The patrol car sat at the kerb, blue-and-whites spinning. A few of the residents stood in their front rooms, ogling out at the spectacle. But none felt the need to step out into the wet to satisfy their curiosity.

Logan brushed his hands on his jeans. 'You've got the photos?'

Wheezy held them up. 'We already did this, Guv.'

'Then we're doing it again, aren't we?' He led the way up the path to the house directly opposite where they'd found Gordy Taylor's body. Leaned on the bell.

A tall woman, stooped forward by a rounding between her shoulder blades, peered out at them with sharp features. 'Yes?'

Wheezy showed her two photos. One from way back, when Gordy was still in the army. A confident young man with a broad smile and shiny eyes, sitting on the bonnet of a military Land Rover. The other photo was from the ID database, the one they used to make books to show witnesses with a height chart in the background – long greasy hair and an unkempt beard, the shiny eyes turned narrow and suspicious, sunken into dark bags. 'You seen this man?'

She barely glanced at the pictures – stared at the patrol car instead. 'Do you have any idea what this is doing to property prices round here? Dead bodies, policemen, *journalists*.' The last word was pronounced as if it smelled of raw sewage.

Wheezy tried again. 'Have you seen him?'

'*Yes*, I *recognize* him. He was the dead tramp they found over there. His face was in the papers. Now if there's nothing else, I've got to get the dinner on.'

Logan stepped a bit closer. The porch was tiny, but it kept some of rain off his head. 'Take another look.'

She shook her head, setting a severe brown bob wobbling. 'Don't need to. It was horrible. I mean the smell, and the shouting, and *oh, my God*, the singing. Well, if you could call that singing, I certainly couldn't. It was like someone drowning parrots in the bath, it really was, and the *language*! Don't speak to me about the language he used.' She sniffed. Snuck a glance at the patrol car. Lowered her voice. 'I know we're not supposed to speak ill of the dead, but he made life unbearable for everyone. I mean, there are people here with small children! Well, it's not wholesome, is it?'

The man in the suit frowned at the photos in Wheezy's hand for a bit, then nodded. 'It's that poor sod, isn't it? The one who drank himself to death behind the bins.' A tut.

164

A wee voice sounded in the hallway behind him. 'Daddy, you're missing *Peppa Pig*!'

He turned. 'I'll be there in a minute, darling. Daddy's speaking to the nice policemen right now.' And back to Logan. 'It's a terrible thing, isn't it? Of course, I blame society. These people don't need Care in the Community, they need proper medical help...'

The woman blinked a couple of times, brushed a strand of grey hair away from her face. Then pulled on her glasses and had a good squint at the photographs, deepening the lines around her eyes. 'Oh dear. He was such a wholesome looking young man.' She took off her glasses and let them dangle on the chain around her neck. Then stared back at Logan. 'I'm so sorry. I really am.'

She didn't glance over his shoulder at the patrol car with its spinning lights. Kept her eyes on Logan instead.

He tilted his head to one side. Why did she look familiar?

Right – she was the nosy old bat pretending to prune her rosebush the first time he was there. The one with the double-glazing van parked outside. The one who'd called the police to complain about Gordy Taylor three times in one week.

'You weren't very happy about him being here, were you, Mrs...?'

'Please, call me Olivia.' A blink. 'And no, I wasn't really. Would you be?'

Logan pulled on his brightest smile. 'Sorry to bother you, Olivia, but is there any chance my Detective Constable could use your toilet? Standing out in the rain, you know how it is.'

She moved to block the door. Then pursed her lips. And pulled on a smile of her own. 'No, of course. Do come in.' She backed away, top lip curling slightly as Logan and

Wheezy Doug stepped over the threshold and dripped on the polished floorboards. 'First on the right.'

The hallway was beige, with a smattering of photographs and a framed poster advertising a railway journey from the fifties. Panel doors. A dado rail.

Wheezy excused himself and squeezed past, into the downstairs loo.

Logan gave it a pause, then clapped his hands together. 'Don't suppose there's any chance of a cup of tea as well?'

The smile brittled. 'Of course. Where are my manners.'

She led him through to an immaculate kitchen. More beige. A large, stripy, ginger cat lay full length along the radiator, tail twitching. The cat turned and peered at him with emerald eyes.

Logan closed the kitchen door. 'Lovely home you have here.'

'Thank you.' The kettle went on, and three china mugs appeared from a cupboard. 'My Ronald was in the building trade for years, so we were able to get a lot of things done.'

A creak from outside, in the corridor. That would be Wheezy going for a poke about.

Logan raised his voice a bit to cover the noise. 'I like the patio doors. Very stylish.'

The white PVC monstrosities overlooked a perfect lawn, lined with perfect bushes, and perfect apple trees groaning with fruit. A nice little seating area, with a wrought-iron table, four chairs, and a barbecue.

'They're French doors, not patio.' She dumped teabags in the mugs. 'Patio doors slide, French doors are hinged.'

'My mistake.' He tried the handle. They weren't locked, so he pulled the door open, letting in the hiss of rain through the leaves. 'Very swish. Look brand new.'

'Yes, well.' She curled her lip again. 'We had to get them replaced.'

'Ah, right.' The only thing *not* perfect about the lawn was the pigeon staggering along the fenceline. One wing flapping, head lolling. 'I saw the glazier's van. Was it an accident?'

The kettle's rumble hit its crescendo, then *click*, it fell silent.

Olivia brought her chin up. 'Someone tried to break in.'

'I see.' He stepped over to the ginger cat and ran a hand along its back. The tail went straight up, then the cat hopped down from its radiator and sauntered towards the open French doors. Paused to stretch with its bum in the air. 'Did you report anything? Any stolen property? Ooh, I don't know … Sleeping pills, painkillers, big bottle of whisky – that kind of thing?'

Her back stiffened. 'I don't think I like your tone.'

Logan nodded toward the mugs. 'Just milk for me, thank you. Detective Constable Andrews is milk and three: he's got a sweet tooth.'

She put the kettle back on its base unit. 'I think I'd like you to go now.'

'What did you do with the empty whisky bottle?' He narrowed his eyes. 'No, let me guess: it went out with the recycling.'

The ginger cat slipped out into the rain and padded across the lawn, making straight for the struggling pigeon.

Colour rushed up Olivia's cheeks. 'Now look what you've done!' She pushed past him, through the patio doors, sandals slapping on the wet paving slabs. 'Paddington! You come back here this instant, young man!'

The cat didn't seem to care. It hunkered down on its front legs, bum wiggling in the air, then pounced.

'NO!' Olivia lunged, but she was too slow to grab Paddington before he crashed his orange-stripy weight down on top of the pigeon. 'Don't you dare eat that!'

Logan stepped out into the garden as she wrestled the pigeon away from her cat.

'Dirty! Bad Paddington!'

An outraged meow, then Paddington turned and stalked off to lurk under the bench by the back wall.

The pigeon may have been half-dead to begin with, but it was all-the-way dead now. It dangled in Olivia's hands, head swaying on the end of its neck like a soggy pendulum.

'Honestly.' She glowered after the cat. 'You *know* these make you sick.' Then Olivia yanked the lid off the dustbin and dumped the dead little body inside. Clanged the lid shut again.

Logan stared at the bin.

Stacey looked up at him, still holding on to his arm. 'If it was me, if I had a cat, I wouldn't want poisoned mice staggering around the house looking to get caught and eaten. Would you?'

'The pigeons make him sick?'

Olivia pulled her shoulders back. 'That's why I don't let Paddington eat them. They're foul little things; who knows where they've been?' She sniffed. 'Why those idiots next door insist on feeding them, is beyond me. They don't even *like* pigeons.'

The idiots next door – Mr Sensitive, with his Peppa Pig obsessed little girl.

Logan crossed to the fence and peered into the adjoining garden.

A bird table poked out of the lawn. Not your standard wee house on a stick, this was a fancy wrought-iron thing with different levels, all suspended around a central pole. One layer had a wide, round base and a pitched roof over it to keep the bird feed dry. Whole wheat birdseed, from the look of it. Whole wheat and bright blue.

He turned and hurried back into the house. Banged his hand on the kitchen door as he barrelled through it. 'WHEEZY! WE'VE GOT THE WRONG HOUSE!'

20

Logan leaned on the bell again while Wheezy dragged the two officers from the patrol car. One blinking and scrubbing at her face as if she'd been catching a nap in the passenger seat.

The door popped open, as they started up the path.

Mr Sensitive pulled on his smile. 'Can I help you?'

Logan wedged his foot in the open door, stopping it from closing. Stared back. 'We know.'

The smile slipped. Then fell. Mr Sensitive licked his lips. 'Really? That's...' He cleared his throat. 'I have no idea what you're talking about.'

'Rat poison and whisky.'

A breath huffed out of him. Then he clicked his mouth shut. Blinked at the police officers looming in front of his house. Swallowed.

The same little voice sounded in the hall behind him. 'Daddy, you're *missing* it!'

Fingers trembled across his lips. 'Oh God...'

'Daddy!'

'I think you'd better come with us, don't you, sir?'

He closed his eyes and swore.

*   *   *

Mark Cameron stared down at his hands – coiled into claws on the interview room table. The skin nearly as pale as the white Formica top. 'Does my daughter have to know?'

Logan shrugged. 'Probably. It's going to be in the papers. On the news. Someone will say something.'

A shudder. 'I don't want her to know.'

The camera lens stared down at them, the red light glaring in judgement.

'Are you sure you don't want a lawyer, Mark?'

A nod.

'For the record, Mr Cameron is nodding his head.'

A deep breath, then he spread his claws. 'That … *man* was hanging out on the street for days. Going through the bins. Shouting. Swearing. Singing. Then one day he pushed Jenny off her bike. Probably didn't do it on purpose, probably too drunk to know *what* he was doing, but he did it.'

Logan folded his arms. 'Is that why you killed him, Mark? Because he hurt Jenny?'

Cameron shook his head. 'I was…' He blinked. Wiped the back of one hand across his eyes. 'We were asleep. Must've been about two in the morning, when there's this crashing noise. And Angie's convinced someone's in the house.'

The digital recorder whirred away to itself.

Outside in the corridor, someone laughed.

A car drove by.

Then Mark Cameron licked his lips. 'So I got up. And it was *him*. Broke one of the conservatory windows and got into our house.' Mark looked away. 'He was outside Jenny's room when I found him and I lost it. I punched him and kicked him and kicked him and stamped on his filthy head…' A shuddering breath. 'I wanted to *kill* him. But I couldn't. Not like that. Not like an animal.'

170

What was probably meant to be a smile twisted Cameron's face. 'So I apologized. I *begged* him not to report me to the police. And I gave him something for the pain – stuff Angie gets for her migraines.'

This time the pause didn't last for nearly as long. 'Only that wasn't enough, was it? Next day he came back demanding more painkillers. And booze. The day after that too. And the next. Every evening, there he'd be with his hand out.' Mark Cameron closed his eyes. 'I couldn't kill him like an animal, because he wasn't an animal – he was *vermin*. And we all know what you use to kill vermin.'

'Well?' DCI Steel was waiting outside Interview Room Number Three, one hand jammed into her armpit, an e-cigarette poking out the corner of her mouth.

Logan closed the interview room door, shutting out the sobbing. Then started down the corridor. 'Didn't have to burst him, he burst himself.'

'He *definitely* killed Gordy Taylor?'

'Got it all on tape.'

'Ya beauty.' She slammed a hand into Logan's back. 'Well done, that man! I'm impressed.'

'I'm going home. Get some unpacking done.'

'Don't be daft.' Steel linked her arm through his, gave it a little squeeze. 'You've got to celebrate! Big win like this calls for something special. Like a bit of quality daddy–daughter time.' A wink. 'Susan's taking me out to see a film. Don't know when we'll be back, but don't wait up, eh? Might get lucky in the back seat of the cinema.'

Logan stopped in the middle of the corridor, stared up at the ceiling and swore. 'I just moved house; I *need* to unpack.' And to sit in the dark for a bit, drinking whisky and trying to figure out what the hell he was going to do about Reuben.

'Nah, what you need's a pizza, a tenner, a bottle of red wine, and to babysit your daughter.' She gave his arm another squeeze. 'You ever watched *Peppa Pig*?'

'Oh God...'

Stuart MacBride

**A *SUNDAY TIMES*
NO.1 BESTSELLER**

**MULTIPLE AWARD-WINNING
AUTHOR**

READ ON TO FIND OUT MORE ABOUT
STUART MACBRIDE'S BESTSELLING NOVELS

'The Logan McRae series is set in Aberdeen, the Granite City, Oil Capital of Europe, perched on the east coast of Scotland. They always say, "write what you know" so I did – using Aberdeen as the backdrop for a series of horrific crimes, murders, serial killers, with much eating of chips and drinking of beer.

Of these, the only ones I have any direct experience of are beer and chips, but some nice local police officers helped me fill in the rest.'

Stuart MacBride

Winter in Aberdeen: murder, mayhem and terrible weather

It's DS Logan McRae's first day back on the job after a year off on the sick, and it couldn't get much worse. Three-year-old David Reid's body is discovered in a ditch: strangled, mutilated and a long time dead. And he's only the first. There's a serial killer stalking the Granite City and the local media are baying for blood.

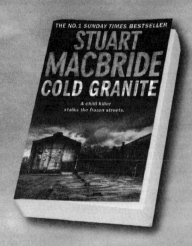

Soon the dead are piling up in the morgue almost as fast as the snow on the streets, and Logan knows time is running out. More children are going missing. More are going to die. If Logan isn't careful, he could end up joining them.

⊙ ebook · audio

It's summertime in the Granite City: the sun is shining, the sky is blue and people are dying...

It starts with Rosie Williams, a prostitute, stripped naked and beaten to death down by the docks – the heart of Aberdeen's red light district. For DS Logan McRae it's a bad start to another bad day.

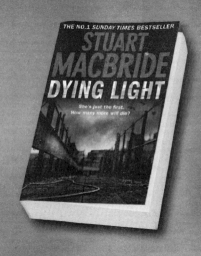

Rosie won't be the only one making an unscheduled trip to the morgue. Across the city six people are burning to death in a petrol-soaked squat, the doors and windows screwed shut from the outside.

And despite Logan's best efforts, it's not long before another prostitute turns up on the slab...

The Granite City's seedy side is about to be exposed...

A serial rapist is leaving a string of tortured women behind him, but while DS Logan McRae's girlfriend, PC Jackie 'Ball Breaker' Watson, is out acting as bait, he's trying to identify a blood-drenched body dumped outside Accident and Emergency.

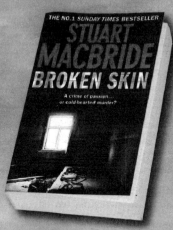

Logan's investigations suggest someone in the local bondage community has developed a taste for violent death, and he soon finds himself dragged into the twilight world of pornographers, sex-shops and S&M.

Meanwhile, the prime suspect in the rape case turns out to be Aberdeen Football Club's star striker. Logan thinks they've got it horribly wrong, but Jackie is convinced the footballer's guilty and she's hell-bent on a conviction at any cost...

⬇ ebook • audio

Panic strikes the Granite City...

When an offshore container turns up at Aberdeen Harbour full of human meat, it kicks off the largest manhunt in the Granite City's history.

Twenty years ago 'The Flesher' was butchering people all over the UK – turning victims into oven-ready joints – until Grampian's finest put him away. But eleven years later he was out on appeal. Now he's missing and people are dying again.

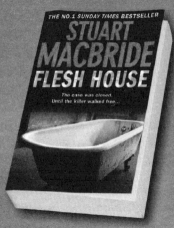

When members of the original investigation start to disappear, Detective Sergeant Logan McRae realizes the case might not be as clear cut as everyone thinks...

Twenty years of secrets and lies are being dragged into the light. And the only thing that's certain is Aberdeen will never be the same again.

'You can't be an eyewitness if I cut out your eyes...'

Someone's preying on Aberdeen's growing Polish population. The pattern is always the same: men abandoned on building sites, barely alive, their eyes gouged out and the sockets burned.

With the victims too scared to talk, and the only witness a paedophile who's on the run, Grampian Police is getting nowhere fast. The attacks are brutal, they keep on happening, and soon DS Logan McRae will have to decide how far he's prepared to bend the rules to get a result.

The Granite City is on the brink of gang warfare; the investigating team are dogged by allegations of corruption; and Logan's about to come to the attention of Aberdeen's most notorious crime lord...

🔽 ebook • audio

Everyone deserves a second chance

Richard Knox has done his time and seen the error of his ways. He wants to leave his dark past behind, so why shouldn't he be allowed to live wherever he wants?

Detective Sergeant Logan McRae isn't thrilled about having to help a violent rapist settle into Aberdeen. Even worse, he's stuck with the man who put Knox behind bars, DSI Danby, supposedly around to 'keep an eye on things'.

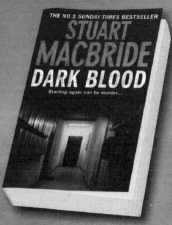

Only things are about to go very, very wrong.

Edinburgh gangster Malk the Knife wants a slice of Aberdeen's latest development boom. Local crime lord Wee Hamish Mowat has ominous plans for Logan's future. And Knox's past isn't finished with him yet...

'You will raise money for the safe return of Alison and Jenny McGregor. You have fourteen days, or Jenny will be killed.'

Aberdeen's own mother-daughter singing sensation are through to the semi-finals of TV smash-hit *Britain's Next Big Star*. But their reality-TV dream has turned into a real-life nightmare. The ransom demand appears in all the papers, on the TV, and the internet, telling the nation to dig deep if they want to keep Alison and Jenny alive. Time is running out, but DS Logan McRae and his colleagues have nothing to go on: the kidnappers haven't left a single piece of forensic evidence and there are no witnesses.

It looks as if the price of fame just got a lot higher...

 ebook · audio

The first body is chained to a stake: strangled and stabbed, with a burning tyre around its neck. A gangland execution or something darker?

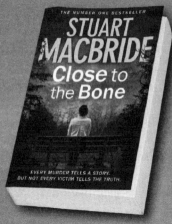

Someone's leaving little knots of bones on DI Logan McRae's doorstep, but he's got bigger concerns. Rival drug gangs are fighting over product and territory; two teenage lovers are missing; and Logan's gained the unwelcome attention of the local crime boss.

When another body turns up, the similarities between these murders and the plot of a bestselling novel seem like more than a coincidence. And perhaps those little knots of bones are more important than they look...

When you catch a twisted killer there should be a reward, right? What DI Logan McRae gets is a 'development opportunity' in rural Aberdeenshire.

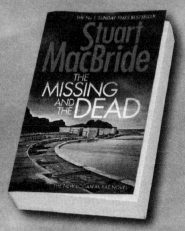

Welcome to divisional policing – catching drug dealers, shop lifters, vandals and the odd escaped farm animal.

Then a little girl's body washes up outside the sleepy town of Banff, kicking off a massive manhunt. Soon the Major Investigation Team is up from Aberdeen, wanting answers. DCI Steel wants Logan back on her team, whether he likes it or not. The top brass are breathing down her neck, and she needs results.

One thing's clear: there are dangerous predators lurking in the wilds of Aberdeenshire, and not everyone's getting out of this alive...

⊕ **ebook • audio**

The Ash Henderson novels

Five years ago DC Ash Henderson's daughter, Rebecca, disappeared on the eve of her thirteenth birthday. A year later the first card arrived: homemade, with a Polaroid stuck to the front. Rebecca, strapped to a chair, gagged and terrified. Every year another card – each one worse than the last.

The tabloids call him 'The Birthday Boy'. He's been snatching girls for years, always just before their thirteenth birthday, killing them slowly, then torturing their families with his homemade cards.

But Ash hasn't told anyone what happened to Rebecca – they think she ran away – because he doesn't want to be taken off the investigation. He's sacrificed too much to give up before his daughter's murderer gets what he deserves...

Eight years ago, 'The Inside Man' murdered four women and left three more in critical condition – all with their stomachs slit open and a plastic doll stitched inside. And then he just ... disappeared.

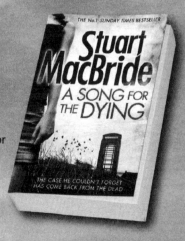

Ash Henderson was a Detective Inspector on the investigation, but a lot has changed since then. His family has been destroyed, his career is in tatters, and one of Oldcastle's most vicious criminals is making sure he spends the rest of his life in prison.

Now a nurse has turned up dead, a plastic doll buried beneath her skin, and it looks as if Ash might finally get a shot at redemption. At earning his freedom. At revenge.

⊕ ebook · audio